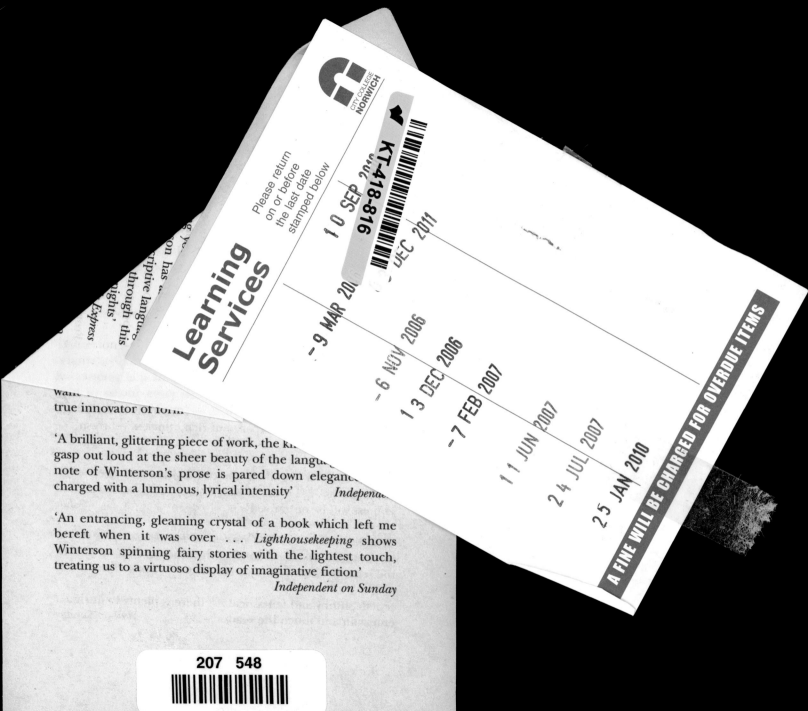

true innovator of form

'A brilliant, glittering piece of work, the ki...
gasp out loud at the sheer beauty of the langu...
note of Winterson's prose is pared down elegan...
charged with a luminous, lyrical intensity'   *Independe...*

'An entrancing, gleaming crystal of a book which left me
bereft when it was over ... *Lighthousekeeping* shows
Winterson spinning fairy stories with the lightest touch,
treating us to a virtuoso display of imaginative fiction'
                                        Independent on Sunday

...on has ...
...riptive langu...
...through this
...ights'
                        Express

...ther
of the I...
magic s...eau...
hypnoti... pared-...
and c...rming'

'*Such* a delight that it seen...
Winterson's writing is incre...
poetry: there is not a superfluou...
for that all too rare a gift – writin...
remember, even memorise ... Winter...
winning combination of slow, languid, des...
and a suspense-filled plot which speed you...
gem, perfect for curling up with on dark, lonely...

Daily...

'A marvellously skilful juggling act of ideas and emotion...
... Winterson's prodigious talent brings the book alive'
JUSTINE PICARDIE, *Evening Standard*

'There is something rare and rather beautiful about
Jeanette Winterson's writing. Never needlessly embellished,
often darkly droll, it is spare but rich; timeless yet fresh'
Time Out

'Delicious ... a beguiling mix of fairy tale and steely emo-
tional truths ... Lovers of kisses, shipwrecks, seahorses and
sadness will be entranced'
Elle

'A sheer delight ... The success of *Lighthousekeeping* lies in
its complete disregard for fact in favour of fantasy, and in
the seductive richness of its language'   *Scotland on Sunday*

'Poetic, funny and fantastical ... there is plenty to intrigue,
entertain and touch the reader'   *Mail on Sunday*

'Rich in language, experimental in form, fierce in its engagement, but it has an elegant simplicity' *Scotsman*

'Structure, content and style all complement each other irresistibly ... *Lighthousekeeping* shows that as a storyteller Winterson still shines tall and true' *Glasgow Herald*

'Assertively written, intricately structured, artful and allusive, thick with Winterson's characteristic word-play, puns on literal and metaphorical meanings' *TLS*

'Fresh and inventive, with many flashes of brilliance ... No one chooses a metaphor as perfectly as Winterson, one of contemporary English literature's most original voices'
Sunday Tribune

By the same author

JEANETTE WINTERSON

Lighthousekeeping

HARPER PERENNIAL
London, New York, Toronto and Sydney

Harper Perennial
An imprint of HarperCollins*Publishers*
77–85 Fulham Palace Road
Hammersmith
London W6 8JB

www.harperperennial.co.uk

This edition published by Harper Perennial 2005
1

First published in Great Britain by Fourth Estate 2004

ISBN 0 00 718150 7

Typeset in New Baskerville

Printed and bound in Great Britain by
Clays Ltd, St Ives plc

'Remember you must die'

MURIEL SPARK

'Remember you must live'

ALI SMITH

TWO ATLANTICS

My mother called me Silver. I was born part precious metal part pirate.

I have no father. There's nothing unusual about that, even children who do have fathers are often surprised to see them. My own father came out of the sea and went back that way. He was crew on a fishing boat that harboured with us one night when the waves were crashing like dark glass. His splintered hull shored him for long enough to drop anchor inside my mother.

Shoals of babies vied for life.

I won.

I lived in a house cut steep into the bank. The chairs had to be nailed to the floor, and we were never allowed to eat spaghetti. We ate food that stuck to the plate – shepherd's pie, goulash, risotto, scrambled egg. We tried peas once – what a disaster – and sometimes we still find them, dusty and green in the corners of the room.

Some people are raised on a hill, others in the valley. Most of us are brought up on the flat. I came at life at an angle, and that's how I've lived ever since.

At night my mother tucked me into a hammock slung cross-wise against the slope. In the gentle sway of the night, I dreamed of a place where I wouldn't be fighting gravity with my own body weight. My mother and I had to rope us together like a pair of climbers, just to achieve our own front door. One slip, and we'd be on the railway line with the rabbits.

'You're not an outgoing type,' she said to me, though this may have had much to do with the fact that going out was such a struggle. While other children were bid farewell with a casual, 'Have you remembered your gloves?' I got, 'Did you do up all the buckles on your safety harness?'

Why didn't we move house?

My mother was a single parent and she had conceived out of wedlock. There had been no lock on her door that night when my father came to call. So she was sent up the hill, away from the town, with the curious result that she looked down on it.

Salts. My home town. A sea-flung, rock-bitten, sand-edged shell of a town. Oh, and a lighthouse.

They say you can tell something of a person's life by observing their body. This is certainly true of my dog. My dog has back legs shorter than his front legs, on account of always digging in at one end, and always scrambling up at the other. On ground level he walks with a kind of bounce that adds to his cheerfulness. He doesn't know that other dogs' legs are the same length all the way round. If he thinks at all, he thinks that every dog is like him, and so he suffers none of the morbid introspection of the human race, which notes every curve from the norm with fear or punishment.

'You're not like other children,' said my mother. 'And if you can't survive in this world, you had better make a world of your own.'

The eccentricities she described as mine were really her own. She was the one who hated going out. She was the one who couldn't live in the world she had been given. She longed for me to be free, and did everything she could to make sure it never happened.

We were strapped together like it or not. We were climbing partners.

And then she fell.

This is what happened.

The wind was strong enough to blow the fins off a fish. It was Shrove Tuesday, and we had been out to buy flour and eggs to make pancakes. At one time we kept our own hens, but the eggs rolled away, and we had the only hens in the world who had to hang on by their beaks while they tried to lay.

I was excited that day, because tossing pancakes was something you could do really well in our house – the steep slope under the oven turned the ritual of loosening and tossing into a kind of jazz. My mother danced while she cooked because she said it helped her to keep her balance.

Up she went, carrying the shopping, and pulling me behind her like an after-thought. Then some new thought must have clouded her mind, because she suddenly stopped and half-turned, and in that moment the wind blew like a shriek, and her own shriek was lost as she slipped.

In a minute she had dropped past me, and I was hanging on to one of our spiny shrubs – escallonia, I think it was, a salty shrub that could withstand the sea

6

and the blast. I could feel its roots slowly lifting like a grave opening. I kicked the toes of my shoes into the sandy bank, but the ground wouldn't give. We were both going to fall, falling away from the cliff face to a blacked-out world.

I couldn't hang on any longer. My fingers were bleeding. Then, as I closed my eyes, ready to drop and drop, all the weight behind me seemed to lift. The bush stopped moving. I pulled myself up on it and scrambled behind it.

I looked down.

My mother had gone. The rope was idling against the rock. I pulled it towards me over my arm, shouting, 'Mummy! Mummy!'

The rope came faster and faster, burning the top of my wrist as I coiled it next to me. Then the double buckle came. Then the harness. She had undone the harness to save me.

Ten years before I had pitched through space to find the channel of her body and come to earth. Now she had pitched through her own space, and I couldn't follow her.

She was gone.

Salts has its own customs. When it was discovered that my mother was dead and I was alone, there was talk of what to do with me. I had no relatives and no father. I had no money left to me, and nothing to call my own but a sideways house and a skew-legged dog.

It was agreed by vote that the schoolteacher, Miss Pinch, would take charge of matters. She was used to dealing with children.

On my first dismal day by myself, Miss Pinch went with me to collect my things from the house. There wasn't much – mainly dog bowls and dog biscuits and a *Collins World Atlas*. I wanted to take some of my mother's things too, but Miss Pinch thought it *unwise*, though she did not say why it was unwise, or why being wise would make anything better. Then she locked the door behind us, and dropped the key into her coffin-shaped handbag.

'It will be returned to you when you are twenty-one,' she said. She always spoke like an Insurance Policy.

'Where am I going to live until then?'

'I shall make enquiries,' said Miss Pinch. 'You may spend tonight with me at Railings Row.'

Railings Row was a terrace of houses set back from the road. They reared up, black-bricked and salt-stained, their paint peeling, their brass green. They had once been the houses of prosperous tradesmen, but it was a long time since anybody had prospered in Salts, and now all the houses were boarded up.

Miss Pinch's house was boarded up too, because she said she didn't want to attract burglars.

She dragged open the rain-soaked marine-ply that was hinged over the front door, and undid the triple locks that secured the main door. Then she let us in to a gloomy hallway, and bolted and barred the door behind her.

We went into her kitchen, and without asking me if I wanted to eat, she put a plate of pickled herrings in front of me, while she fried herself an egg. We ate in complete silence.

'Sleep here,' she said, when the meal was done. She placed two kitchen chairs end to end, with a cushion on one of them. Then she got an eiderdown out of the cupboard – one of those eiderdowns that have more feathers on the outside than on the inside, and one of those eiderdowns that were only stuffed with one duck. This one had the whole duck in there I think, judging from the lumps.

So I lay down under the duck feathers and duck feet and duck bill and glassy duck eyes and snooked duck tail, and waited for daylight.

We are lucky, even the worst of us, because daylight comes.

The only thing for it was to advertise.

Miss Pinch wrote out all my details on a big piece of paper, and put it up on the Parish notice board. I was free to any caring owner, whose good credentials would be carefully vetted by the Parish Council.

I went to read the notice. It was raining, and there was nobody about. There was nothing on the notice about my dog, so I wrote a description of my own, and pinned it underneath:

ONE DOG. BROWN AND WHITE ROUGH
COATED TERRIER. FRONT LEGS 8 INCHES
LONG. BACK LEGS 6 INCHES LONG.
CANNOT BE SEPARATED.

Then I worried in case a person might mistake it was the dog's legs that could not be separated, instead of him and me.

'You can't force that dog on anybody,' said Miss Pinch, standing behind me, her long body folded like an umbrella.

'He's my dog,'

'Yes, but whose are you? That we don't know, and not everybody likes dogs.'

Miss Pinch was a direct descendent of the Reverend Dark. There were two Darks – the one who lived here, that was the Reverend, and the one who would rather be dead than live here, that was his father. Here you meet the first one, and the second one will come along in a minute.

Reverend Dark was the most famous person ever to come out of Salts. In 1859, a hundred years before I was born, Charles Darwin published his *Origin of Species*, and came to Salts to visit Dark. It was a long story, and like most of the stories in the world, never finished. There was an ending – there always is – but the story went on past the ending – it always does.

I suppose the story starts in 1814, when the Northern Lighthouse Board was given authority by an Act of Parliament to 'erect and maintain such additional lighthouses upon such parts of the coast and islands of Scotland as they shall deem necessary'.

At the north-western tip of the Scottish mainland is a wild, empty place, called in Gaelic *Am Parbh* – the Turning Point. What it turns towards, or away from, is unclear, or perhaps it is many things, including a man's destiny.

The Pentland Firth meets the Minch, and the Isle of Lewis can be seen to the west, the Orkneys to the east, but northwards there is only the Atlantic Ocean. I say only, but what does that mean? Many things, including a man's destiny.

The story begins now – or perhaps it begins in 1802

11

when a terrible shipwreck lobbed men like shuttlecocks into the sea. For a while, they floated cork up, their heads just visible above the water line, but soon they sank bloated like cork, their rich cargo as useless to life as their prayers.

The sun came up the next day and shone on the wreck of the ship.

England was a maritime nation, and powerful business interests in London, Liverpool and Bristol demanded that a lighthouse be built here. But the cost and the scale were enormous. To protect the Turning Point, a light needed to be built at Cape Wrath.

Cape Wrath. Position on the nautical chart, 58° 37.5° N, 5°W.

Look at it – the headland is 368 feet high, wild, grand, impossible. Home to gulls and dreams.

There was a man called Josiah Dark – here he is – a Bristol merchant of money and fame. Dark was a small, active, peppery man, who had never visited Salts in his life, and on the day that he did he vowed never to return. He preferred the coffee-houses and conversation of easy, wealthy Bristol. But Salts was the place that would provide the food and the fuel for the lighthousekeeper and his family, and Salts would have to provide the labour to build it.

So with much complaining and more reluctance, Dark bedded for a week at the only inn, The Razorbill.

It was an uncomfortable place; the wind screeched at the windows, a hammock was half the price of a bed, and a bed was twice the price of a good night's sleep. The food was mountain mutton that tasted like fencing, or hen tough as a carpet, that came flying in, all a-squawk behind the cook, who smartly broke its neck.

Every morning Josiah drank his beer, for they had no coffee in this wild place, and then he wrapped himself tight as a secret, and went up onto Cape Wrath.

Kittiwakes, guillemots, fulmars and puffins covered the headland, and the Clo Mor cliffs beyond. He thought of his ship, the proud vessel sinking under the black sea, and he remembered again that he had no heir. He and his wife had produced no children and the doctors regretted they never would. But he longed for a son, as he had once longed to be rich. Why was money worth everything when you had none of it, and nothing when you had too much?

So, the story begins in 1802, or does it really begin in 1789, when a young man, as fiery as he was small, smuggled muskets across the Bristol Channel to Lundy Island, where supporters of the Revolution in France could collect them.

He had believed in it all, somewhere he did still, but his idealism had made him rich, which was not what he intended. He had intended to escape to France with his mistress and live in the new free republic. They would be rich because everyone in France was going to be rich.

When the slaughtering started, he was sickened. He was not timid of war, but the tall talk and the high hearts had not been for this, this roaring sea of blood.

To escape his own feelings, he joined a ship bound for the West Indies and returned with a 10% share in the treasure. After that, everything he did increased his wealth.

Now he had the best house in Bristol and a lovely wife and no children.

As he stood still as a stone pillar, an immense black gull landed on his shoulder, its feet gripping his wool coat. The man dared not move. He thought, wildly, that the bird would carry him off like the legend of the eagle and child. Suddenly, the bird spread its huge wings and flew straight out over the sea, its feet pointed behind it.

When the man got to the inn, he was very quiet at his dinner, so much so that the wife of the establishment began to question him. He told her about the bird, and she said to him, 'The bird is an omen. You must build your lighthouse here as other men would build a church.'

But first there was the Act of Parliament to be got,

then his wife died, then he took sail for two years to repair his heart, then he met a young woman and loved her, and so much time passed that it was twenty-six years before the stones were laid and done.

The lighthouse was completed in 1828, the same year as Josiah Dark's second wife gave birth to their first child.

Well, to tell you the truth, it was the same day.

The white tower of hand-dressed stone and granite was 66 feet tall, and 523 feet above the sea at Cape Wrath. It had cost £14,000.

'To my son!' said Josiah Dark, as the light was lit for the first time, and at that moment Mrs Dark, down in Bristol, felt her waters break, and out rushed a blue boy with eyes as black as a gull. They called him Babel, after the first tower that ever was, though some said it was a strange name for a child.

The Pews have been lighthousekeepers at Cape Wrath since the day of the birth. The job was passed down generation to generation, though the present Mr Pew has the look of being there forever. He is as old as a unicorn, and people are frightened of him because he isn't like them. Like and like go together. Likeness is liking, whatever they say about opposites.

But some people are different, that's all.

I look like my dog. I have a pointy nose and curly hair. My front legs – that is, my arms, are shorter than my back legs – that is, my legs, which makes a symmetry with my dog, who is just the same, but the other way round.

His name's DogJim.

I put up a photo of him next to mine on the notice board, and I hid behind a bush while they all came by and read our particulars. They were all sorry, but they all shook their heads and said, 'Well, what could we do with her?'

It seemed that nobody could think of a use for me, and when I went back to the notice board to add something encouraging, I found I couldn't think of a use for myself.

Feeling dejected, I took the dog and went walking, walking, walking along the cliff headland towards the lighthouse.

Miss Pinch was a great one for geography – even though she had never left Salts in her whole life. The way she described the world, you wouldn't want to visit it anyway. I recited to myself what she had taught us about the Atlantic Ocean …

The Atlantic is a dangerous and unpredictable ocean. It is the second largest ocean in the world, extending in an S shape from the Arctic to the Antarctic regions, bounded by North and South America in the West, and Europe and Africa in the East.

The North Atlantic is divided from the South Atlantic by the equatorial counter-current. At the Grand Bank off Newfoundland, heavy fogs form where the warm Gulf Stream meets the cold Labrador Current. In the North Western Ocean, icebergs are a threat from May to December.

Dangerous. Unpredictable. Threat.

The world according to Miss Pinch.

But, on the coasts and outcrops of this *treacherous* ocean, a string of lights was built over 300 years.

Look at this one. Made of granite, as hard and unchanging as the sea is fluid and volatile. The sea moves constantly, the lighthouse, never. There is no sway, no rocking, none of the motion of ships and ocean.

Pew was staring out of the rain-battered glass; a silent taciturn clamp of a man.

Some days later, as we were eating breakfast in Railings Row – me, toast without butter, Miss Pinch, kippers and tea – Miss Pinch told me to wash and dress quickly and be ready with all my things.

'Am I going home?'

'Of course not – you have no home.'

'But I'm not staying here?'

17

'No. My house is not suitable for children.'

You had to respect Miss Pinch – she never lied.

'Then what is going to happen to me?'

'Mr Pew has put in a proposal. He will apprentice you to lighthousekeeping.'

'What will I have to do?'

'I have no idea.'

'If I don't like it, can I come back?'

'No.'

'Can I take DogJim?'

'Yes.'

She hated saying *yes*. She was of those people for whom *yes* is always an admission of guilt or failure. *No* was power.

A few hours later, I was standing on the windblown jetty, waiting for Pew to collect me in his patched and tarred mackerel boat. I had never been inside the lighthouse before, and I had only seen Pew when he stumped up the path to collect his supplies. The town didn't have much to do with the lighthouse any more. Salts was no longer a seaman's port, with ships and sailors docking for fire and food and company. Salts had become a hollow town, its life scraped out. It had its rituals and its customs and its past, but nothing left in it was alive. Years ago, Charles Darwin had called it

Fossil-Town, but for different reasons. Fossil it was, salted and preserved by the sea that had destroyed it too.

Pew came near in his boat. His shapeless hat was pulled over his face. His mouth was a slot of teeth. His hands were bare and purple. Nothing else could be seen. He was the rough shape of human.

DogJim growled. Pew grabbed him by the scruff and threw him into the boat, then he motioned for me to throw in my bag and follow.

The little outboard motor bounced us over the green waves. Behind me, smaller and smaller, was my tipped-up house that had flung us out, my mother and I, perhaps because we were never wanted there. I couldn't go back. There was only forward, northwards into the sea. To the lighthouse.

Pew and I climbed slowly up the spiral stairs to our quarters below the Light. Nothing about the lighthouse had been changed since the day it was built. There were candleholders in every room, and the Bibles put there by Josiah Dark. I was given a tiny room with a tiny window, and a bed the size of a drawer. As I was not much longer than my socks, this didn't matter. DogJim would have to sleep where he could.

Above me was the kitchen where Pew cooked

sausages on an open cast-iron stove. Above the kitchen was the light itself, a great glass eye with a Cyclops stare.

Our business was light, but we lived in darkness. The light had to be kept going, but there was no need to illuminate the rest. Darkness came with everything. It was standard. My clothes were trimmed with dark. When I put on a sou'wester, the brim left a dark shadow over my face. When I stood to bathe in the little galvanised cubicle Pew had rigged for me, I soaped my body in darkness. Put your hand in a drawer, and it was darkness you felt first, as you fumbled for a spoon. Go to the cupboards to find the tea caddy of Full Strength Samson, and the hole was as black as the tea itself.

The darkness had to be brushed away or parted before we could sit down. Darkness squatted on the chairs and hung like a curtain across the stairway. Sometimes it took on the shapes of the things we wanted: a pan, a bed, a book. Sometimes I saw my mother, dark and silent, falling towards me.

Darkness was a presence. I learned to see in it, I learned to see through it, and I learned to see the darkness of my own.

Pew did not speak. I didn't know if he was kind or unkind, or what he intended to do with me. He had lived alone all his life.

That first night, Pew cooked the sausages in darkness. No, Pew cooked the sausages *with* darkness. It was the kind of dark you can taste. That's what we ate: sausages and darkness.

I was cold and tired and my neck ached. I wanted to sleep and sleep and never wake up. I had lost the few things I knew, and what was here belonged to somebody else. Perhaps that would have been all right if what was inside me was my own, but there was no place to anchor.

There were two Atlantics; one outside the lighthouse, and one inside me.

The one inside me had no string of guiding lights.

A beginning, a middle and an end is the proper way to tell a story. But I have difficulty with that method.

Already I could choose the year of my birth – 1959. Or I could choose the year of the lighthouse at Cape Wrath, and the birth of Babel Dark – 1828. Then there was the year Josiah Dark first visited Salts – 1802. Or the year Josiah Dark shipped firearms to Lundy Island – 1789.

And what about the year I went to live in the lighthouse – 1969, also the year that Apollo landed on the moon?

I have a lot of sympathy with that date because it felt like my own moon landing; this unknown barren rock that shines at night.

There's a man on the moon. There's a baby on earth. Every baby plants a flag here for the first time.

So there's my flag – 1959, the day gravity sucked me out of the mother-ship. My mother had been in labour for eight hours, legs apart in the air, like she was skiing through time. I had been drifting through the unmarked months, turning slowly in my weightless world. It was the light that woke me; light very different to the soft silver and night-red I knew. The light called me out – I remember it as a cry, though you will say that was mine, and perhaps it was, because a baby knows no separation between itself and life. The light *was* life. And what light is to plants and rivers and animals and seasons and the turning earth, the light was to me

When we buried my mother, some of the light went out of me, and it seemed proper that I should go and live in a place where all the light shone outwards and none of it was there for us. Pew was blind, so it didn't matter to him. I was lost, so it didn't matter to me.

Where to begin? Difficult at the best of times, harder when you have to begin again.

Close your eyes and pick another date: 1 February 1811.

This was the day when a young engineer called Robert Stevenson completed work on the lighthouse at Bell Rock. This was more than the start of a lighthouse; it was the beginning of a dynasty. For 'lighthouse' read

24

'Stevenson'. They built scores of them until 1934 and the whole family was involved, brothers, sons, nephews, cousins. When one retired, another was immediately appointed. They were the Borgias of lighthouse-keeping.

When Josiah Dark went to Salts in 1802, he had a dream but no one to build it. Stevenson was still an apprentice – lobbying, passionate, but without any power and with no record of success. He started out on Bell Rock as an assistant, and gradually took over the project that was hailed as one of the 'modern wonders of the world'. After that, everybody wanted him to build their lighthouses, even where there was no sea. He became fashionable and famous. It helps.

Josiah Dark had found his man. Robert Stevenson would build Cape Wrath.

There are twists and turns in any life, and though all of the Stevensons should have built lighthouses, one escaped, and that was the one who was born at the moment Josiah Dark's son, Babel, made a strange reverse pilgrimage and became Minister of Salts.

1850 – Babel Dark arrives in Salts for the first time.

1850 – Robert Louis Stevenson is born into a family of prosperous civil engineers – so say the innocent annotated biographical details – and goes on to write *Treasure Island, Kidnapped, The Strange Case of Dr Jekyll and Mr Hyde.*

The Stevensons and the Darks were almost related, in fact they were related, not through blood but through the restless longing that marks some individuals from others. And they were related because of a building. Robert Louis came here, as he came to all his family lighthouses. He once said, 'Whenever I smell salt water, I know I am not far from one of the works of my ancestors.'

In 1886, when Robert Louis Stevenson came to Salts and Cape Wrath, he met Babel Dark, just before his death, and some say it was Dark, and the rumour that hung about him, that led Stevenson to brood on the story of Jekyll and Hyde.

'What was he like, Pew?'

'Who, child?'

'Babel Dark.'

Pew sucked on his pipe. For Pew, anything to do with thinking had first to be sucked in through his pipe. He sucked in words, the way other people blow out bubbles.

'He was a pillar of the community.'

'What does that mean?'

'You know the Bible story of Samson.'

'No I don't.'

'Then you've had no right education.'

'Why can't you just tell me the story without starting with another story?'

'Because there's no story that's the start of itself, any more than a child comes into the world without parents.'

'I had no father.'

'You've no mother now neither.'

I started to cry and Pew heard me and was sorry for what he had said, because he touched my face and felt the tears.

'That's another story yet,' he said, 'and if you tell yourself like a story, it doesn't seem so bad.'

'Tell me a story and I won't be lonely. Tell me about Babel Dark.'

'It starts with Samson,' said Pew, who wouldn't be put off, 'because Samson was the strongest man in the world and a woman brought him down, then when he was beaten and blinded and shorn like a ram he stood between two pillars and used the last of his strength to bring them crashing down. You could say that Samson was two pillars of the community, because anyone who sets himself up is always brought down, and that's what happened to Dark.

'The story starts in Bristol in 1848 when Babel Dark was twenty years old and as rich and fine as any gentleman of the town. He was a ladies' man, for all that he was studying Theology at Cambridge, and everyone said he would marry an heiress from the Colonies and take up his father's business in ships and trade.

'It was set fair to be so.

'There was a pretty girl lived in Bristol and all the town knew her for her red hair and green eyes. Her father was a shopkeeper, and Babel Dark used to visit the shop to buy buttons and braids and soft gloves and neckties, because I have said, haven't I, that he was a bit of a dandy?

'One day – a day like this, yes just like this, with the sun shining, and the town bustling, and the air itself like a good drink – Babel walked into Molly's shop, and spent ten minutes examining cloth for riding breeches, while he watched out of the corner of his eye until she had finished serving one of the Jessop girls with a pair of gloves.

'As soon as the shop was empty, Babel swung over to the counter and asked for enough braid to rig a ship, and when he had bought all of it, he pushed it back towards Molly, kissed her direct on the lips, and asked her to a dance.

'She was a shy girl, and Babel was certainly the handsomest and the richest young man that paraded the waterfront. At first she said no, and then she said yes, and then she said no again, and when all the yeas and nays had been bagged and counted, it was unanimous by a short margin, that she was going to the dance.

'His father didn't disapprove, because old Josiah was no snob, and his own first love had been a jetty girl, back in the days of the French Revolution.'

'What's a jetty girl?'

'She helps with the nets and the catch and luggage and travellers and so on, and in the winter she scrapes the boats clean of barnacles and marks the splinters for tarring by the men. Well, as I was saying, there were no obstacles to the pair meeting when they liked, and the thing continued, and then, they say, and this is all rumour and never proved, but they say that Molly found herself having a child, and no legal wedded father.'

'Like me?'

'Yes, the same.'

'It must have been Babel Dark.'

'That's what they all said, and Molly too, but Dark said not. Said he wouldn't and couldn't have done such a thing. Her family asked him to marry her, and even Josiah took him aside and told him not to be a panicky fool, but to own up and marry the girl. Josiah was all for buying them a smart house and setting up his son straight away, but Dark refused it all.

'He went back to Cambridge that September, and when he came home at Christmas time, he announced his intention of going into the Church. He was dressed all in grey, and there was no sign of his bright waistcoats and red top boots. The only thing he still wore from his former days was a ruby and emerald pin that he had bought very expensive when he first took up with Molly O'Rourke. He'd given her one just like it for her dress.

'His father was upset and didn't believe for a minute that he had got to the bottom of the story, but he tried to make the best of it, and even invited the Bishop to dinner, to try and get a good appointment for his son.

'Dark would have none of it. He was going to Salts.

"Salts?" said his father. "That God-forsaken sea-claimed rock?'

'But Babel thought of the rock as his beginning, and it was true that as a child his favourite pastime when it rained was to turn over the book of drawings that Robert Stevenson had made, of the foundations, the column, the keeper's quarters, and especially the prismatic diagrams of the light itself. His father had never taken him there, and now he regretted it. One week at The Razorbill would surely have been enough for life.

'Well, it was a wet and wild and woebegone January when Babel Dark loaded two trunks onto a clipper bound seaward from Bristol and out past Cape Wrath.

'There were plenty of good folks to see him go, but Molly O'Rourke wasn't amongst them because she had gone to Bath to give birth to her child.

'The sea smashed at the ship like a warning, but she made good headway, and began to blur from view, as we watched Babel Dark, standing wrapped in black, looking at his past as he sailed away from it forever.'

'Did he live in Salts all his life?'

'You could say yes, and you could say no.'

'Could you?'

'You could, depending on what story you were telling.'

'Tell me!'

'I'll tell you this – what do you think they found in his drawer, after he was dead?'

'Tell me!'

'Two emerald and ruby pins. Not one – two.'

'How did he get Molly O'Rourke's pin?'

'Nobody knows.'

'Babel Dark killed her!'

'That was the rumour, yes, and more.'

'What more?'

Pew leaned close, the brim of his sou'wester touching mine. I felt his words on my face.

'That Dark never stopped seeing her. That he married her in secret and visited her hidden and apart under another name for both of them. That one day, when their secret would have been told, he killed her and others besides.'

'But why didn't he marry her?'

'Nobody knows. There are stories, oh yes, but nobody knows. Now off to bed while I tend the light.'

Pew always said 'tend the light', as though it were his child he was settling for the night. I watched him moving round the brass instruments, knowing everything by touch, and listening to the clicks on the dials to tell him the character of the light.

'Pew?'

'Go to bed.'

'What do you think happened to the baby?'

'Who knows? It was a child born of chance.'

'Like me?'

'Yes, like you.'

I went quietly to bed, DogJim at my feet because there was nowhere else for him. I curled up to keep warm, my knees under my chin, and hands holding my toes. I was back in the womb. Back in the safe space before the questions start. I thought about Babel Dark, and about my own father, as red as a herring. That's all I know about him – he had red hair like me.

A child born of chance might imagine that Chance was its father, in the way that gods fathered children, and then abandoned them, without a backward glance, but with one small gift. I wondered if a gift had been left for me. I had no idea where to look, or what I was looking for, but I know now that all the important journeys start that way.

KNOWN POINT IN
THE DARKNESS

As an apprentice to lighthouse-keeping my duties were as follows:

1) Brew a pot of Full Strength Samson and take it to Pew.
2) 8 am. Take DogJim for a walk.
3) 9 am. Cook bacon.
4) 10 am. Sluice the stairs.
5) 11 am. More tea.
6) Noon. Polish the instruments.
7) 1 pm. Chops and tomato sauce.
8) 2 pm. Lesson – History of Lighthouses.
9) 3 pm. Wash our socks etc.
10) 4 pm. More tea.
11) 5 pm. Walk the dog and collect supplies.
12) 6 pm. Pew cooks supper.
13) 7 pm. Pew sets the light. I watch.
14) 8 pm. Pew tells me a story.
15) 9 pm. Pew tends the light. Bed.

Numbers 3, 6, 7, 8 and 14 were the best times of the day. I still get homesick when I smell bacon and Brasso.

Pew told me about Salts years ago, when wreckers lured ships onto the rocks to steal the cargo. The weary seamen were desperate for any light, but if the light is a lie, everything is lost. The new lighthouses were built to prevent this confusion of light. Some of them lit great fires on their platforms, and burned out to sea like a dropped star. Others had only twenty-five candles, standing in the domed glass like a saint's shrine, but for the first time, the lighthouses were mapped. Safety and danger were charted. Unroll the paper, set the compass, and if your course is straight, the lights will be there. What flickers elsewhere is a trap or a lure.

The lighthouse is a known point in the darkness.

'Imagine it,' said Pew, 'the tempest buffeting you starboard, the rocks threatening your lees, and what saves you is a single light. The harbour light, or the warning light, it doesn't matter which; you sail to safety. Day comes and you're alive.'

'Will I learn to set the light?'

'Aye, and tend the light too.'

'I hear you talking to yourself.'

'I'm not talking to myself, child, I'm about my work.' Pew straightened up and looked at me seriously. His eyes were milky blue like a kitten's. No one knew whether or not he had always been blind, but he had spent his whole life in the lighthouse or on the mackerel boat, and his hands were his eyes.

'A long time ago, in 1802 or 1892, you name your date, there's most sailors could not read nor write. Their officers read the navy charts, but the sailors had their own way. When they came past Tarbert Ness or Cape Wrath or Bell Rock, they never thought of such places as positions on the map, they knew them as stories. Every lighthouse has a story to it – more than one, and if you sail from here to America, there'll not be a light you pass where the keeper didn't have a story for the seamen.

In those days the seamen came ashore as often as they could, and when they put up at the inn, and they had eaten their chops and lit their pipes and passed the rum, they wanted a story, and it was always the lighthousekeeper who told it, while his Second or his wife stayed with the light. These stories went from man to man, generation to generation, hooped the sea-bound world and sailed back again, different decked maybe, but the same story. And when the lightkeeper had told his story, the sailors would tell their own, from other lights. A good keeper was one who knew more stories than the sailors. Sometimes there'd be a competition, and a salty dog would shout out "Lundy" or "Calf of Man" and you'd have to answer, "*The Flying Dutchman*" or "*Twenty Bars of Gold*".'

Pew was serious and silent, his eyes like a faraway ship.

'I can teach you – yes, anybody – what the instruments are for, and the light will flash once every four seconds as it always does, but I must teach you how to keep the light. Do you know what that means?'

I didn't.

'The stories. That's what you must learn. The ones I know and the ones I don't know.'

'How can I learn the ones you don't know?'

'Tell them yourself.'

Then Pew began to say of all the sailors riding the waves who had sunk up to their necks in death and found one last air pocket, reciting the story like a prayer.

'There was a man close by here, lashed himself to a spar as his ship went down, and for seven days and seven nights he was on the sea, and what kept him alive while others drowned was telling himself stories like a madman, so that as one ended another began. On the seventh day he had told all the stories he knew and that was when he began to tell himself as if he were a story, from his earliest beginnings to his green and deep misfortune. The story he told was of a man lost and found, not once, but many times, as he choked his way out of the waves. And when night fell, he saw the Cape Wrath light, only lit a week it was, but it was, and he knew that if he became the story of the light, he might be saved. With his last strength he began to paddle towards it, arms on either side of the spar, and in his mind the light became a shining rope, pulling him in. He took hold of it, tied it round his waist, and at that moment, the keeper saw him, and ran for the rescue boat.

'Later, putting up at The Razorbill, and recovering, he told anyone who wanted to listen what he had told himself on those sea-soaked days and nights. Others joined in, and it was soon discovered that every light had a story – no, every light *was* a story, and the flashes themselves were the stories going out over the waves, as markers and guides and comfort and warning.'

Cliff-perched, wind-cleft,

the church seated 250, and was almost full at 243 souls, the entire population of Salts.

On 2 February 1850, Babel Dark preached his first sermon.

His text was this: 'Remember the rock whence ye are hewn, and the pit whence ye are digged.'

The innkeeper at The Razorbill was so struck by this sermon and its memorable text that he changed the name of his establishment. From that day forth, he was no longer landlord of The Razorbill, but keeper of The Rock and Pit. Sailors, being what they are, still called it by its former name for a good sixty years or more, but The Rock and Pit it was, and is still, with much the same low-beamed, inward-turned, net-hung, salt-dashed, sea-weed feel of forsakenness that it always had.

Babel Dark used his private fortune to build himself a fine house and a walled garden and to equip himself comfortably there. He was soon seen in earnest Biblical discussion with the one lady of good blood in the place – a cousin of the Duke of Argyll, a Campbell in exile, out of poverty and some other secret. She was no beauty, but she read German fluently and knew something of Greek.

They were married in 1851, the year of the Great Exhibition, and Dark took his new wife to London for her honeymoon, and thereafter he never took her anywhere again, not even to Edinburgh. Wherever he went, riding alone on a black mare, no one was told, and no one followed.

There were disturbances at night, sometimes, and the Manse windows all flamed up, and shouts and hurlings of furniture or heavy objects, but question Dark, as few did, and he would say it was his soul in peril, and he fought for it, as every man must.

His wife said nothing, and if her husband was gone for days at a time, or seen wandering in his black clothes over the high rocks, then let him be, for he was a Man of God, and he accepted no judge but God himself.

One day, Dark saddled his horse and disappeared.

He was gone a month, and when he returned, he was softer, easier, but with plain sadness on his face.

After that, the month-long absences happened twice a year, but no one knew where he went, until a Bristol man put up at The Razorbill, that is to say The Rock and Pit.

He was a close-guarded man, eyes as near together as to be always spying on one another, and a way of tapping his finger and thumb, very rapid, when he spoke. His name was Price.

One Sunday, after Price had been to church, he was sitting over the fire with a puzzlement on his face, and it was finally got out of him that if he hadn't seen Babel Dark before and just recently, then the man had the devil's imprint down in Bristol.

Price claimed that he had seen Dark, wearing very different clothes, visiting a house in the Clifton area outside Bristol. He took note of him for his height – tall, and his bearing – very haughty. He had never seen him with anyone, always alone, but he would swear on his tattoo that this was the same one.

'He's a smuggler,' said one of us.

'He's got a mistress,' said another.

'It's none of our business,' said a third. 'He does his duties here and he pays his bills and handsomely. What else he does is between him and God.'

The rest of us were not so sure, but as nobody had the money to follow him, none of us could know whether Price's story was true or not. But Price promised to keep a look out, and to send word, if he ever saw Dark or his like again.

'And did he?'

'Oh yes, indeed he did, but that didn't help us to know what Dark was about, or why.'

'You weren't there then. You weren't born.'

'There's always been a Pew in the lighthouse at Cape Wrath.'

'But not the same Pew.'

Pew said nothing. He put on his radio headphones, and motioned me to look out to sea. 'The *McCloud*'s out there,' he said.

I got the binoculars and trained them on a handsome cargo ship, white on the straight line of the horizon. 'She's the most haunted vessel you'll ever see.'

'What haunts her?'

'The past,' said Pew. 'There was a brig called the *McCloud* built two hundred years ago, and that was as wicked a ship as sailed. When the King's navy scuttled her, her Captain swore an oath that he and his ship would some day return. Nothing happened until they built the new *McCloud*, and on the day they launched her, everyone on the dock saw the broken sails and ruined keel of the old *McCloud* rise up in the body of the ship. There's a ship within a ship and that's fact.'

'It's not a fact.'

'It's as true as day.'

I looked at the *McCloud*, fast, turbined, sleek, computer-controlled. How could she carry in her body the trace-winds of the past?

'Like a Russian doll, she is,' said Pew, 'one ship inside another, and on a stormy night you can see the old *McCloud* hanging like a gauze on the upper deck.'

'Have you seen her?'

'Sailed in her and seen her,' said Pew.

'When did you board the new *McCloud*? Was she in dry dock at Glasgow?'

'I never said anything about the new *McCloud*,' said Pew.

'Pew, you are not two hundred years old.'

'And that's a fact,' said Pew, blinking like a kitten. 'Oh yes, a fact.'

'Miss Pinch says I shouldn't listen to your stories.'

'She doesn't have the gift, that's why.'

'What gift?'

'The gift of Second Sight, given to me on the day I went blind.'

'What day was that?'

'Long before you were born, though I saw you coming by sea.'

'Did you know it would be me, me myself as I am, me?'

Pew laughed. 'As sure as I knew Babel Dark – or someone very like me knew someone very like him.'

I was quiet. Pew could hear me thinking. He touched my head, in that strange, light way of his, like a cobweb.

'It's the gift. If one thing is taken away, another will be found.'

'Miss Pinch doesn't say that, Miss Pinch says Life is a Steady Darkening Towards Night. She's embroidered it above her oven.'

'Well, she never was the optimistic kind.'

'What can you see with your Second Sight?'

'The past and the future. Only the present is dark.'

'But that's where we live.'

'Not Pew, child. A wave breaks, another follows.'

'Where's the present?'

'For you, child, all around, like the sea. For me, the sea is never still, she's always changing. I've never lived on land and I can't say what's this or that. I can only say what's ebbing and what's becoming.'

'What's ebbing?'

'My life.'

'What's becoming?'

'Your life. You'll be the keeper after me.'

Tell me a story, Pew.

What kind of story, child?
A story with a happy ending.
There's no such thing in all the world.
As a happy ending?
As an ending.

To make an end of it Dark had decided to marry.

His new wife was gentle, well read, unassuming, and in love with him. He was not in the least in love with her, but that, he felt, was an advantage.

They would both work hard in a parish that fed on oatmeal and haddock. He would hew his path, and if his hands bled, so much the better.

They were married without ceremony in the church at Salts, and Dark immediately fell ill. The honeymoon had to be postponed, but his new wife, all tenderness and care, made him breakfast every day with her own hands, though she had a maid to do it for her.

He grew to dread the hesitant tread on the stairs to his room that overlooked the sea. She carried the tray so slowly that by the time she reached his room the tea had gone cold, and every day she apologised, and every day he told her to think nothing of it, and swallowed a sip or two of the pale liquid. She was trying to be economical with the tea leaves.

That morning, he lay in bed and heard the clinking of the cups on the tray, as she came slowly towards him. It would be porridge, he thought, heavy as a mistake, and muffins studded with raisins that accused him as he ate them. The new cook – her appointment – baked bread plain, and disapproved of 'fanciness' as she called it, though what was fancy about a raisin, he did not know.

He would have preferred coffee, but coffee was four times the price of tea.

'We are not poor,' he had said to his wife, who reminded him that they could give the money to a better cause than breakfast coffee.

Could they? He was not so sure, and whenever he saw a deserving lady with a new bonnet, it seemed to smell, to him, steamingly aromatic.

The door opened, she smiled – not at him, at the tray – because she was concentrating. He thought, irritably, that a tightrope walker he had seen on the docks would have carried this tray with more grace and skill, even on a line strung between two masts.

She set it down, with her usual air of achievement and sacrifice.

'I hope you will enjoy it, Babel,' she said, as she always did.

He smiled and took the cold tea.

Always. They had not been married long enough for there to be an always.

They were new, virgin, fresh, without habits. Why did he feel that he had lain in this bed forever, slowly filling up with cold tea?

Till death us do part.

He shivered.

'You are cold, Babel,' she said.

'No, only the tea.'

She looked hurt, rebuked.

'I make the tea before I toast the muffins.'

'Perhaps you should do it afterwards.'

'Then the muffins would be cold.'

'They are cold.'

She picked up the tray. 'I will make us a second breakfast.'

It was as cold as the first. He did not speak of it again.

He had no reason to hate his wife. She had no faults and no imagination. She never complained, and she was never pleased. She never asked for anything, and she never gave anything – except to the poor. She was modest, mild-mannered, obedient, and careful. She was as dull as a day at sea with no wind.

In his becalmed life, Dark began to taunt his wife, not out of cruelty at first, but to test her, perhaps to find her. He wanted her secrets and her dreams. He was not a man of good mornings and good nights.

When they went out riding, he would sometimes thrash her pony with a clean sing of his whip, and the beast would gallop off, his wife grabbing the mane because she was an uncertain horsewoman. He liked the pure fear in her face – a feeling at last, he thought.

He took her sailing on days when Pew would have been a brave man to take out his rescue boat. Dark liked to watch her, drenched and vomiting, begging him to steer home and when they got the boat back, half capsized with water, he'd declare it a fine day's sailing, and make her walk to the house holding his hand.

In the bedroom, he turned her face down, one hand against her neck, the other bringing himself stiff, then he knocked himself into her in one swift move, like a wooden peg into the tap-hole of a barrel. His finger-marks were on her neck when he had finished. He never kissed her.

When he wanted her, which was never as herself, but sometimes, because he was a young man, he trod slowly up the stairs to her room, imagining he was carrying a tray of greasy muffins and a pot of cold tea. He opened the door, smiling, but not at her.

When he had finished with her, he sat across her, keeping her there, the way he would keep his dog down when he went out shooting. In the chilly bedroom – she never lit a fire – he let his semen go cold on her before he let her get up.

Then he went and sat in his study, legs flung up on the desk, thinking of nothing. He had trained himself to think of absolutely nothing.

On Wednesday afternoons, they visited the poor. He loathed it; the low houses, mended furniture, women patching clothes and nets with the same needle and the same coarse twine. The houses smelled of herrings and smoke. He did not understand how any person could live in such wretchedness. He would rather have ended his life.

His wife sat sympathetically listening to stories of no wood, no eggs, sore gums, dead sheep, sick children, and always she turned to him as he stood brooding out of the window, and said, 'The pastor will offer you a word of comfort.'

He would not turn round. He murmured something about Jesus's love and left a shilling on the table.

'You were hard, Babel,' his wife said as they walked away.

'Shall I be a hypocrite, like you?'

That was the first time he hit her. Not once, but again and again and again, shouting, 'You stupid slut, you stupid slut, you stupid slut.' Then he left her swollen and bleeding on the cliff path and ran back to the Manse and into the scullery, where he knocked the lid off the copper and plunged both his hands up to their elbows in the boiling water.

He held them there, crying out, as the skin reddened and began to peel, then with the skin white and bubbled on his fingers and palms, he went outside and began to chop wood until his wounds bled.

For several weeks, he avoided his wife. He wanted to say he was sorry, and he was sorry, but he knew he would do it again. Not today or tomorrow, but it would break out of him, how much he loathed her, how much he loathed himself.

In the evenings she read to him from the Bible. She liked reading the miracles, which surprised him in someone whose nature was as unmiraculous as a bucket. She was a plain vessel who could carry things; tea trays, babies, a basket of apples for the poor.

'What apples?' he asked

She had broken off reading and was talking about apples.

'The ones you brought with you wrapped in newspaper. It is time they were eaten up. I will stew them, and take them to the poor.'

'No.'

'What is the reason?'

'They are from my father's tree.'

'The tree will fruit again.'

'No. It never will.'

His wife paused a moment. She could see his agitation, but she did not understand it. She began to speak, then left off, and took up her magnifying glass and began to read the story of Lazarus.

Dark wondered what it must be like to lie in the tomb, airless and silent, without light, hearing voices far off.

'Like this,' he thought.

How can a man become his own death, choose it, take it, have no one to blame but himself? He had refused life. Well then, he would have to make what he could of this death.

The next day he began to write it all down. He kept two journals; the first, a mild and scholarly account of a clergyman's life in Scotland. The second, a wild and torn folder of scattered pages, disordered, unnumbered, punctured where his nib had bitten the paper.

He taught himself to wait until he had finished his sermon, and then he took out the leather folder and the stained pages, and wrote his life. It was not a life that anyone around him would have recognised. As time passed, he no longer recognised himself.

Free me, he wrote one night, but to whom?

Then, hardly knowing what he did, he decided to take his wife to London for the Great Exhibition. She had no wish to go, but she thought it better not to cross him.

TENANT OF THE SUN

The moon shone the night white.

Pew and I were sitting in The Razorbill, that is to say, The Rock and Pit.

There was nobody else there. Pew had a key to The Rock and Pit, and he liked to go drinking on Saturday night, because, he said, that's what Pews had always done. Until I came to live with him, he had let himself in, and drunk alone from a barrel of rum behind the bar so thick with dust that if you stood a glass on the top of it, the glass sank like a ghost ship in the fog.

I was given a packet of crisps on Saturday nights, even though Miss Pinch had warned that it might lead to trouble, though she did not say what kind of trouble. The trouble seemed to be me.

I had met her earlier in the day, as I was pushing our

sack truck along the pot-holed road to the town. Her hand hung over me like one of those mechanical grabbers in scrapyards. She said she was Disappointed that I hadn't been to school, and that this would Hinder my Progress. Immediately I thought of a bright blue boat beaten back by the waves. How could I be both the boat and the waves? This was very deep.

'You are not listening to me,' she said.

'I am. It was the storm. We couldn't leave the lighthouse.'

'Captain Scott was not discouraged by the weather,' said Miss Pinch. 'He reached the South Pole in spite of the snow.'

'But he died in his tent!'

'Death, where is thy sting?'

I had no idea.

'Take this,' she said. 'I have borrowed it from the Mobile Library.'

It was a copy of Captain Scott's diaries.

I began to read it while I was waiting for Pew. *I do not regret this journey … We took risks … These rough notes must tell the tale.*

I looked at the pictures of them, lost in their white-coloured nowhere.

'Why did they die, Pew?'

'They lost heart, child. Amundsen had beaten them to it, and when it came to the return, they had no fight left in them. You must never lose heart.'

'No?'

'No.'

The moon was rising, full and clear and polar-white. The Introduction to the diaries told me that Scott had wanted to go to the Pole because there were so few adventures left. The world was nearly mapped in 1913. No one ever thought that in 1968 someone would go to the moon.

'Do you see her?' said Pew. 'I can feel her the way the sea feels her. She pulls at me like the sea. That's how I know when there will be a storm.'

I was thinking of Captain Scott, lying in his snowy ocean waste, the white moon on his face, and if he dreamed of being there – a place as cold as this, as remote, as beautiful, as unlikely.

Not earth-bound any more, he could wing the dogs in a wind-ruff of fur, husky-haloed through two miles or so of gravity, then out, free, barking at the moon, half-wolf, half-tame, going home to the white planet he had seen shining in their orange eyes, paws hock-deep in snow.

No one knows what happens at the end of the journey. No one knows where the dead go.

Pew and I had gone inside, and we were sitting side by side as we always did, staring straight ahead, as we always did. The electricity had long since been disconnected. You might think it a grave of a place, but not Pew.

'Every table was full,' said Pew, 'and the men were three-deep at the bar.

'Some nights, Dark himself would come in, and the men made room for him to sit alone, where we sit now, and then the talk would dry up like a harbour at low tide, although Dark looked at no man and spoke to no man.

'He brought his Bible with him, and it was always his own story he read – not that you would know it, being so poorly brought up – but the story he read was of the first Tower of Babel in the book of Genesis.

'That tower was built as high as the moon, so that the people who built it could climb up and be like God. When it came shattering down, the people were scattered to the ends of the earth, and they no more understood each other's language than they understood the language of fishes and birds.

'I said to him one day, "Why do you read that story, Minister?" He said to me, "Pew, I have become a stranger in my own life."'

'Did he say that, Pew?'

'He did, child, certain as you and I sit here tonight.'

'You weren't born then.'

'Was I not?'

'And you couldn't see his Bible because you are blind.'

Logic never had any effect on Pew.

'A stranger in his own life, he said, and the fire blazing up, and the men with their backs to him like a sea wall, and a mist outside the place, a mist thick as doubt, and the moon hidden, for all that she was full. He loved the moon, did Babel Dark. My barren rock, he called her, and said sometimes that he would be happy there, pale tenant of the sun.'

'Did he say that?'

'Pale tenant of the sun. I never forgot.'

'How old are you, Pew?'

Pew said nothing. Drank up his rum and said nothing. Then we carefully washed that one remaining glass under the one remaining cold tap, put the glass back on the one remaining woodworm-eaten shelf, and left it there, gleaming in the moonlight that shone through the window, before we walked slowly down the cinder-track to the lighthouse.

The door was his body.

Dark woke out of his sleeping nightmare and into his waking nightmare.

He had dreamed of a door closing and closing.

He woke, his hand on his stomach, his fingers aware of the tip of his erection. He moved his hand outside of the sheets.

It was early. He could hear someone downstairs cleaning out a fire-grate.

He let his mind drift out to sea, imagining Molly lying next to him. In Bristol, he had always woken first; he had trained himself to wake first, so that he could have the first moment of the day looking at her as she slept. He liked to draw his hand out from under the warm sheet, and into the cold air of the bedroom. Then he would hover his hand over the outline of her face, never touching her, but sensing with wonder, always with wonder, how his hand in the cold air could feel the warmth coming off her face.

Sometimes she opened her mouth to breathe, and he felt the breath of her on him, the way Adam must have felt God breathing first life into his sleeping body.

But she was the one who slept. In the little death, he bent to kiss her and wake her, waking her with a kiss, so that her eyes opened sleepily, and she smiled at him.

She always smiled at him. He loved that.

And then he would take her in his arms, burying his face in her neck, and trying to identify all the different smells of her. She was clean but she smelled of herself, something like new hay with the flowers still in it, and something greener, sharper; nettles in the cut hay.

And apples, he thought, the white flesh and its faint pinkness.

When they had first met, he had taken her apple picking in his father's garden. They had propped the ladder, spread the cloth on the ground, and he had been in shirt-sleeves, showing off by climbing higher and higher to get the ones she pointed at, the ones most out of reach.

They had picked nearly the whole tree, and in the afternoon, under the branches of the tree, they sat side by side sorting the best eaters, the best keepers, the apples for jelly, and those apples to be stewed right away, their brown parts cut out with a sharp knife.

He was so aware of her next to him that his hands shook slightly as he pared and slit. She noticed this, because she liked his hands – the long fingers and squared nails.

Then the knife slipped, and he cut his ring finger, and straight away she had taken the knife from him, and chopped a ribbon from her dress to staunch the bleeding.

They had gone inside to find cold water. The kitchen was empty. She knew what to do, and soon she had him clean and bandaged.

'Kiss it better,' she said, bending her head like a bird drinking.

They looked at each other and didn't move at all. Dark was conscious of the sunlight in stencilled squares on the stone floor, and the brightness of the sun through the thick glass, and the sun in her eyes, flecking the pupils, and shining on her as though the sun were showing him a secret door.

He put out his hand and touched her face.

Two days later they made love.

She had asked that it should be dark.

'Like a bed trick,' she had said, though this made him feel uneasy.

Measure for measure, he made his way to her house, showing no light at any window. He used his fingertips and the moon to find the door latch, and as he went in, he saw a lighted candle, in a holder, waiting for him on the bottom step of the wide wooden staircase. He took the candle and went slowly upstairs. He had no idea where he was going. He had never been to this house before.

His footsteps creaked on the landing. He startled a mouse on wainscot business. There were two oil paintings of a man and a woman in blue clothes, and a chest at the end of the corridor. By the chest, he thought he saw an open door. He went towards it.

'Babel?'

'Yes.'

His heart was beating. He was sweating. His groin was tight.

'Put the candle on the chest.'

He did as he was told, and stepped into the dark room, lit only by a few low-burnt coals in the grate. The room was warm. The fire must have been lit for a long time and allowed to burn down.

He could see the bed.

'Molly?'

'Yes.'

'Shall I take off my clothes?'

'Yes.'

His top coat and waistcoat were easy enough. He pulled at his stock and tore it on the pin. His fingers had grown thick and clumsy, and he couldn't undo the flap on his breeches. He didn't curse or speak. He fought in silence with his reluctant outer skin, until he was in his stockings and shirt. Then he went to the bed.

He stood, hesitating, smiling, terrified. Molly sat up, her hair round her shoulders, and falling onto her breasts. Suddenly he was glad it was dark.

She took his shirt and helped him pull it over his head, and then she stared, frankly, at where he stood, raised, ready, unable to hide himself now.

She touched his sides with both hands, running her hands down over his buttocks and thighs, liking his firmness, and kissing his abdomen with her lips. She was confident and certain, while he sweated with desire and fear. Why was she so sure? He wondered, just for a second, if he was the first man who had come to her like this. Then he pushed the thought away and held her close to him.

They made love

Stomach to stomach, mouth on mouth, his feet across her shins and wrapped under her feet. Her hands on his back. His hands stroking her ears, his forearms on either side of her shoulders, like the forepaws of a hound. He could smell her excitement, and he bent his head to kiss the bolts of her collarbone.

He was in her, fused to her spine, so that the tip of him felt every vertebra, it seemed. He counted her to himself, travelling upwards, into her mouth, so that she could speak him. She said his name – *Babel*. Travelling upwards so that he could lie behind her eyes and peep at the world through her. He looked at himself through her eyes – his neck, his chest, his eyes full of love. Was this him – through her eyes? Gentle, ardent, hesitant a little, his skin unwritten but filling up with this new language?

She turned him over. She sat across him. All of him was still. He let her move on him, and he didn't understand when she took his hand and began to use his thumb, just above where he entered her. He let his hand be taught, and later, lying back, she taught him again, with his fingers this time. He was excited, happy, and when she fell asleep, he propped himself on one elbow, uncovering her, stroking her, memorising what he had learned.

And then the thought came again, like a bell out at sea getting closer; a warning bell, a ship arriving in the fog. Yes, he could see it clearly now.

He had not been her first lover.

What other lovers did she have? What other beds burned in dark rooms?

He did not sleep.

Tell me the story, Pew.

What story, child?

The story of Babel Dark's secret.

It was a woman.

You always say that.

There's always a woman somewhere, child; a princess, a witch, a stepmother, a mermaid, a fairy godmother, or one as wicked as she is beautiful, or as beautiful as she is good.

Is that the complete list?

Then there is the woman you love.

Who's she?

That's another story.

GREAT EXHIBITION

This way to the Cobra. Wonders of the East!

It was 1851 and they were in Hyde Park.

Dark felt like a man raised from the dead.

He loved the noise, the excitement, the programme sellers, the postcard sellers, the unofficial stalls, the rogues in red neck-cloths, all chicanery and tongue-twisting. There were card sharps, jugglers, arias from the Italian opera, sign writers who would paint your name next to a gaudy impression of the Crystal Palace. There were miniature train sets that pulled wagons of dolls, and there were women dressed up as dolls, selling violets, selling buns, selling themselves. There were hawkers on boxes offering *the best, the finest, the one and only,* and there were girls who walked on their hands.

There were horses in heavy gear drawing beer barrels, and a man with a panther offering the Mystery

77

of India, and all this before they had queued to enter the Crystal Palace to see the wonders of the Empire.

It was their honeymoon, Dark and his new wife, though their honeymoon had had to be postponed because Dark had fallen ill as soon they had been married.

Now he was well, and wearing his Man of God clothes, he was respectfully motioned through wherever he went.

His wife was tired – she preferred life plain – and so Dark found her a chair and went to fetch each of them pork pies and lemonade. The Queen had been seen eating a pork pie, and suddenly they were fashionable. Rich and poor alike were eating penny pork pies.

Dark had paid his money, and was balancing the pies and the stoppered lemonade bottles, when he heard someone say his name – 'Babel'.

The voice was soft, but it cut him cleanly, the way dressed stone is cut cleanly, and part of him fell away, and what was underneath was rough and unworked.

'Molly,' said Dark, as evenly as he could, but his voice was edged. She was wearing a green dress, her red hair wound in a plait. She was carrying a baby who put her hand out to Dark's face.

Dark hesitated with his cargo and lemonade and pies. Would she sit down with him for a moment?

She nodded.

They went to a series of tables underneath a spread of palm trees brought from India, and as strange and heady to London as a primeval forest. They sat in rattan chairs, while an Indian waiter in a turban and sash served Coronation Chicken to a family of coal merchants from Newcastle.

'Is the baby …?

'She is quite well, Babel, but she is blind.'

'Blind?'

And he was back in that terrible day, when she had come to him, soft and helpless, and he had …

She had another lover – he had always known it. He had watched her walking quickly at night to a house on the other side of town. She was cloaked, shrouded, she hadn't wanted to be seen.

When she had gone in, Dark had stood outside the window. A young man came forward. She held out her arms. The man and Molly embraced. Dark had turned away, the pain in his head sharp in the brain-pan. He had felt his fear drop anchor in the soft parts of him. This was the fear that had been sailing towards him through the fog.

He had set off back to town. He didn't expect to sleep. Soon he began to walk all night. He couldn't remember when he had last slept.

He remembered laughing, and thinking that if he never slept he would be dead. Yes, he felt dead. He felt thin and empty like a dredged shell. He looked in the mirror and saw a highly polished abalone, its inhabitant gone, the shell prized for its surface. He always dressed well.

Molly had noticed the change in him. She tried to please him, and sometimes he could forget, but then, making love, at the moment when he was most naked, he heard the bell again, and sensed the ribbed ship with its ragged sails coming nearer.

He had never told her how he shadowed her steps, and when they had met one night at an inn called Ends Meet, and she had told him she was going to have a child, he had pushed her away and run through the town and locked himself in his rooms, wrapped in ragged sails.

On the walls of his rooms were the drawings that Stevenson had made of the lighthouse at Cape Wrath. The lighthouse looked like a living creature, standing upright on its base, like a seahorse, fragile, impossible, but triumphant in the waves.

'My seahorse,' Molly had called him, when he swam towards her in their bed like an ocean of drowning and longing.

The sea cave and the seahorse. It was their game.

Their watery map of the world. They were at the beginning of the world. A place before the flood.

She had come to him that day, soft, open, as he sat motionless by his dying fire. She had begged him and he had hit her, hit two red coals into her cheeks, and then hit her again and again, and she had put up her arms to shield herself, and …

She broke his thought as she spoke.

'From where I fell.'

He looked at the child, laughing, gurgling, unseeing, its hands on its mother's face, its head turning to follow the sounds. Now he knew what he had done, and he would have given his life to put his hand inside time and turn it back.

'I will do anything you ask. Tell me. Anything.'

'We have no wants.'

'Molly – am I her father?'

'She has no father.'

Molly stood up to leave. Babel jumped after her, spilling the bottles of lemonade. Molly held the baby close, and the baby was quiet, feeling its mother's alarm.

'Let me hold her.'

'So that you can dash her to the ground?'

'I have thought of you every day since I left. And I have thought of your child. Our child, if you tell me so.'

'I did tell you so.'

'I never thought I would see you again.'

'Nor I you.'

She paused, and he remembered her that night, that first night, with the moon shining white on her white skin. He put out his hand. She stepped back.

'It is too late, Babel.'

Yes, too late, and he had made it too late. He should go back, he knew his wife would be waiting for him. He should go back now. But as he took a deep breath to go, his will failed him.

'Spend this day with me. This one day.'

Molly hesitated a long time, while the crowds passed about them, and Dark, looking down, not daring to look up, saw reflections in the polished toe-pieces of his boots.

She spoke like someone far off. Someone who was a country where he was born.

'This day then.'

He shone. She made him shine. He took the baby and held it by the hissing engines, and close against the smooth traction of the wheels. He wanted her to hear pistons pumping and coal shovelling and water drumming against the sides of the giant copper boilers. He took her tiny fingers and ran them over brass rivets, steel funnels, cogs, ratchets, a rubber horn that trumpeted when she squeezed it in her tiny hands, Dark's hands over hers. He wanted to make for her a world of sounds that was as splendid as the world of sight.

Some hours later, he saw Molly smile.

Late now. Crowds were drifting towards the bandstand. Dark bought the baby a clockwork bear made of real bearskin. He rubbed it against her cheek, then he wound it up and the bear brought two cymbals together in its paws.

It was time for him to go, he knew it was, but still they stood together, as everyone else parted to pass them. Then silently, without him asking, Molly opened her bag and gave him a card with her address in Bath.

She kissed his cheek, and turned away.

Dark watched her go, like watching a bird on the horizon, that only you can see, because only you have followed it.

Then she was gone.

Late now. Shadows. The flare of gas lamps. His reflection in every pane of glass. One Dark. A hundred. A thousand. This fractured man.

Dark remembered his wife.

He pushed his way down the galleries and back to where he had left her. She was still there, hands folded in her lap, her face a mask.

'I am sorry,' he said, 'I was delayed.'

'For six hours.'

'Yes.'

Pew – why didn't my mother marry my father?

She never had time. He came and went.

Why didn't Babel Dark marry Molly?

He doubted her. You must never doubt the one you love.

But they might not be telling you the truth.

Never mind that. You tell them the truth.

What do you mean?

You can't be another person's honesty, child, but you can be your own.

So what should I say?

When?

When I love someone?

You should say it.

A stranger in his own life,

but not here, not with her.

The house he bought her in her name. The child he took as his own; his blind daughter, blue-eyed like him, black-haired like him. He loved her.

He promised himself that he would come back forever. He told Molly that what had begun as a penance had become a responsibility. He couldn't leave Salts, not now, no, not yet, but soon, yes very soon. And Molly, who had begged to come with him, accepted what he said about his life there, and that it would be no life for their daughter, and no place for the second child that Molly was expecting.

He said nothing to her about his wife in Salts, and nothing to her about his salty new son, who had been born almost without him noticing.

April. November. The twice-yearly visits to Molly. Sixty days a year where life is, where love is, where his private planet tracked into the warmth of its sun.

In April and November, he arrived half frozen, hardly able to speak, the life in him remote. He came to her door and fell inside, and she took him by the fire and talked to him, for hours it seemed, to keep him conscious, to keep him from fainting.

Whenever he saw her he wanted to faint. He knew it was the sudden rush of blood to his head, and the fact that he forgot to breathe. He knew it was an ordinary symptom and an ordinary cause, but he knew, too, that whenever he saw her, his desiccated, half-stilled body jerked forward, towards the sun. Heat and light. She was heat and light to him, whatever the month.

In December and May, when it was time for him to leave, he carried the light with him for a while, though the source was gone. As he travelled out of the long sun-spread days, he hardly noticed that the clock was shortening, that night was falling earlier, that some mornings there was already a frost.

She was a bright disc in him that left him sun-spun. She was circular, light-turned, equinox-sprung. She was season and movement, but he had never seen her cold. In winter, her fire sank from the surface to below the surface, and warmed her great halls like the legend of the king who kept the sun in his hearth.

'Keep me by you,' he said. It was almost a prayer, but like most of us he prayed for one thing, and set his life on course for elsewhere.

They were in the garden raking leaves. He leaned on his rake and looked at her, their tiny daughter on all fours, feeling the different-shaped edges of the leaves. He picked one up and felt it himself; hornbeam it was, serrated, corrugated, nothing like the fronds of the ash, or the flat, spotted, palm-sized curling sycamore, or the oak, sporting acorns and still green.

He wondered how many days he had in his life – in his whole life – and when they had fallen one by one, and him naked again, time's covering gone, would the leaves be heaped up, the rotting pile of his days, or would he recognise them still – those different-edged days he had called his life?

He put his hand into the pile. This one, and this one – when he had taken Molly and their daughter to the sea. This one, when they had gone for a walk along the beach and he had found her a shell snail-tracked like the inside of an ear. This one, when he had been waiting for her, and when he had seen her before she had seen him, and he was able to watch her, as only strangers can and lovers long to do.

This one, when he had held his baby high above the

world, and perhaps for the first time in his life wanted nothing for himself.

He counted out sixty leaves and arranged them in two blocks of thirty. Well, there were three hundred and sixty-five days in a year. For three hundred and five he would no longer exist.

Why? Why must he live like this? He had got himself caught in a lie and the lie had got him caught in a life. He must finish his sentence. Seven years, he had privately decided when Molly had agreed to take him back.

Then they would leave England forever. He would marry her. His wife and son in Salts would be well provided for. He would be free. No one would ever hear of Babel Dark again.

How were you born, Pew?

Unexpectedly, child. My mother was gathering clams on the sea edge when a handsome enough rogue offered to tell her fortune. As such a thing didn't happen every day, she wiped her hands on her skirt and held out her palm.

Did he see riches, or a great house, or a long life, or a quiet hearth?

He couldn't be sure of any of that, no, but he did foresee a fine child born within nine months of this day.

Really?

Well, she was very perplexed by that, but the fine rogue assured her that the very same thing has happened to Mary, and she had given birth to Our Lord. And after that they took a walk along the beach. And after that she forgot all about him. And after that, his fortune-telling came true.

Miss Pinch says you came from the orphanage in Glasgow.

There's always been a Pew at Cape Wrath.

But not the same Pew.

Well, well.

As I was no longer Making Progress, I let my mind drift where it would. I rowed my blue boat out to sea and collected stories like driftwood. Whenever I found something – a crate, a gull, a message in a bottle, a shark bloated belly-up, pecked and pitted, a pair of trousers, a box of tinned sardines, Pew asked me the story, and I had to find it, or invent it, as we sat through the sea-smashed nights of winter storms.

A crate! Raft for a pygmy sailing to America.

A gull! A princess trapped in the body of a bird.

A message in a bottle. My future.

A pair of trousers. Belonging to my father.

Tinned sardines. We ate those.

Shark. And inside it, dull with blood, a gold coin. Omen of the unexpected. The buried treasure is always there.

When Pew sent me to bed, he gave me a match to light my candle. In the tiny oval of the match flame, he asked me to tell him what I saw – a boy's face, or a horse, or a ship, and as the match burned down, the story would burn out over my fingers and disappear. They were never finished, these stories, always beginning again – the boy's face, a hundred lives, the horse, flying or enchanted, the ship sailing over the edge of the world.

And then I would try to sleep and dream of myself, but the message in the bottle was hard to read.

'Blank,' said Miss Pinch, when I told her about it.

But it wasn't blank. Words were there all right. I could see one of them. It said LOVE.

'That's lucky,' said Pew. 'Lucky to find it. Lucky to search for it.'

'Have you ever loved anybody, Pew?'

'Pew has, yes, child,' said Pew.

'Tell me the story.'

'All in good time. Now go to sleep.'

And I did, the message in the bottle floating just above my head. LOVE, it said. *Love, love, love,* or was it a bird I heard in the night?

The mystery of Pew was a mercury of fact.

Try and put your finger on the solid thing and it scattered into separate worlds.

He was just Pew; an old man with a bag of stories under his arm, and a way of cooking sausages so that the skin turned as thick as a bullet casing, and he was, too, a bright bridge that you could walk across, and look back and find it vanished.

He was and he wasn't – that was Pew.

There were days when he seemed to have evaporated into the spray that jetted the base of the lighthouse, and days when he was the lighthouse. It stood, Pew-shaped, Pew-still, hatted by cloud, blind-eyed, but the light to see by.

DogJim was asleep on his peg rug, made out of scraps like himself. I had unhooked the big brass bell we used to call each other for supper or a story, and I was rubbing the salt off it with a duster torn out of an old vest.

Everything in the lighthouse was old – except me – and Pew was the oldest thing of all, if you believed him.

Pew lit his pipe, and cupped the bowl in both hands, looking up, as the wind-once-a-week ship's clock struck nine.

'Babel Dark lived two lives, child, as I have said. He built Molly a fine house outside Bristol – not too near, but near enough, as though he had to court danger as he courted his new wife – and new wife she was, for Dark married Molly in a thirteenth-century Cornish church, hewn from a single rock.

'Remember the rock whence ye are hewn? Aye, but he had forgotten about the pit.

'Down south, Dark went by the name of Lux and spoke with a Welsh accent, because his mother was Welsh, and he knew the lilt.

'Mr Lux paid well and lived well when he was with Molly, and Molly explained to anyone who was curious that her husband was a man with shipping interests that kept him away for most of the year, except for the two months, April and November, when he came back to her.

'He gave no orders to her but one, that she should never follow him to Salts.

'One day, a handsome woman came and lodged at The Razorbill – that is to say, The Rock and Pit – and gave her name as Mrs Tenebris. She did not state her business, but she went to church on Sunday, as you would expect a lady to do.

'She sat in the front pew in a grey dress, and Dark mounted the pulpit to preach his sermon, and the text was, 'I have set my Covenant in the Heavens like a Bow,' referring to the rainbow after the Flood, when God promised Noah not to destroy the world again – I tell you this, Silver, because your Bible reading is so poor.

'Well, as he spoke, and he was a fine preacher, suddenly he glanced down to the front row, and saw the lady in grey, and those about him said he turned as pale as a skinned plaice. He never faltered in his speaking, but his hands gripped the Bible as though a fiend was dragging it from him.

'As soon as the service was over, he didn't wait to receive anyone at the church door, he took his horse and rode off.

'They saw him, wandering on the cliff edge with his

dog, and they were afraid. He was that kind of man. There was something behind his eyes that made them afraid.

'A week went by, and when the next Sunday came the lady had gone, but she had left something behind in Dark, and that's a fact. You could see his torment written right across him. He used to vex the sailors for their tattoos, but he was the marked man now.'

'Was it Molly?'

'Oh it was her, it was. They had a meeting together, here in this lighthouse, in this very room, her sitting in the chair that I sit in now – him pacing, pacing, pacing, and the rain hammering at the glass like a thing trying to get in.'

'What did they talk about?'

'I only heard some of it – I was outside, of course.'

'Pew, you weren't born.'

'Well, the Pew that was born was.'

'What did she say to him?'

Dark could feel the familiar pain behind his eyes. His eyes were bars, and behind them was a fierce, unfed animal. When people looked at him they had the feeling of being shut out. He did not shut them out. He shut himself in.

He opened the small door at the base of the

lighthouse and climbed round and round the steps to the light. He climbed swiftly and the stairs were steep, but he was hardly out of breath at all. His body seemed to get stronger as his grip on himself lessened. He was in control, yes, he was in control, until he slept, or until his mind escaped his cage as it sometimes did. He had been able to stop it by force of will, just as he had been able to wake up at will, driving the dreams back into the night, lighting his lamp and reading. He had been able to force it all away, and if he woke exhausted in the morning he did not care. But lately, he could never wake out of those dreams. Little by little, the night was winning.

He walked purposefully into the room. He faltered. He stopped. Molly was there, with her back to him, and as she turned round, he loved her. It was very simple; he loved her. Why had he made it so complicated?

'Babel …'

'Why have you come here? I asked you never to follow me.'

'I wanted to see your life.'

'I have no life, but for my life with you.'

'You have a wife and son.'

'Yes.'

He paused. How to explain? He had not lied to Molly – she knew he was the Minister of Salts. It had never seemed necessary to tell her about his wife or his son.

There had been no more children. Couldn't she understand?

'What will you do now?'

'I have not the least idea.'

'I love you,' he said.

The three most difficult words in the world.

She touched him as she went past him and slowly down the stairs. He listened until he heard the door close a long way off – at the bottom of his life, it seemed.

Then he started to cry.

That day in the lighthouse

she had gone up into the light, and in her copper-coloured dress, and autumn hair, she stood like a delicate lever amongst the instruments that revolved and refracted the lens.

This was Babel's beginning, she thought, the reason for his being, the moment of his birth. Why could he not be as steady and as bright?

She had never depended on him, but she had loved him, which was quite different. She had tried to absorb his anger and his uncertainty. She had used her body as a grounding rod. She had tried to earth him. Instead, she had split him.

If she had refused to see him that day, if she had not even spoken his name, if she had seen him and hidden in the crowds, if she had climbed up onto the iron gallery and watched him. If she had never bound up his finger. If she had not lit a fire in a cold room.

He was like this lighthouse in some ways. He was lonely and aloof. He was arrogant, no doubt of that, and cloaked in himself. He was dark. Babel Dark, the light in him never lit. The instruments were in place, and polished too, but the light was not lit.

If she had never lit a fire in a cold room …

But, when she slept or when she was alone, when the children were quiet, her mind spread round him like the sea. He was always present. He was her navigation point. He was the coordinate of her position.

She did not believe in destiny, but she believed in this rocky place. The lighthouse, Babel. Babel, the lighthouse. She would always find him, he would be there, and she would row back to him.

Can you leave someone and be with them? She thought you could. She knew that whatever happened today, whatever action they took, whether she kept him or lost him, it hardly made any difference. She had a feeling of someone in a play or a book. There was a story: the story of Molly O'Rourke and Babel Dark, a beginning, a middle, an end. But there was no such story, not that could be told, because it was made of a length of braid, an apple, a burning coal, a bear with a drum, a brass dial, his footsteps on the stone stairs coming closer and closer.

Dark opened the door.

She did not turn round.

Eyes like a faraway ship, Pew was sleeping.

After I had walked the dog and made the first pot of Full Strength Samson, I sat out on the deck of the light, and started to go through the post. Post was my job because Pew couldn't read it.

There were the usual things – brass instrument catalogues, special offer oilskin coats, thermal underwear from Wolsey – the suppliers of Captain Scott's 1913 Polar Expedition. I put a tick by a maroon vest and longjohns, and opened the last long white envelope.

It was from Glasgow. The lighthouse was going to be automated in six months.

When I read the letter to Pew, he stood up very dignified and threw the ends of his tea into the sea. Gulls screamed round the top of the Light.

'There's been a Pew here since 1828.'

'They're going to give you a lot of money when you leave. It's called a Redundancy Package, and it includes Alternative Accommodation.'

'I don't need money, child. I need what I have. You write to them and tell them that Pew is staying. They can stop paying me, but I'm staying where I am.'

So I wrote a letter to the Northern Lighthouse Board, and they replied, very formally, that Mr Pew would leave on the appointed day, and there would be no right of appeal.

Everything happened as it always does; there was a petition, there were letters in the newspapers, there was a small item on the television news, a picket in Glasgow, then after what was called a period of 'consultation' the Board went ahead as it had planned.

Miss Pinch came visiting, and asked me what I intended to do with my Future. She spoke about it as though it were an incurable disease.

'You have a future,' she said. 'We must take it into account.'

She suggested I try for a Junior Trainee Assistant Librarian Temporary Grade on a three-month work placement. She warned me that I shouldn't be too ambitious – not suitable for Females, but that librarianship was suitable for Females. Miss Pinch always said Females, holding the word away from her by its tail.

My future had been the lighthouse. Without the lighthouse, I would have to begin again – again.

'Isn't there anything else I could do?' I asked Miss Pinch.

'Very unlikely.'

'I'd like to work on a ship.'

'That would be itinerant.'

'My father was crew on a ship.'

'And look what happened to him.'

'We don't know what happened to him.'

'We know he was your father.'

'You mean I happened to him?'

'Exactly. And look how difficult that has been.'

Miss Pinch approved of automation. There was something about human beings that made her uncomfortable. She had refused to sign our petition. Salts, she said, must move with the times, which seemed odd to me, when Miss Pinch had never moved at all – not with the times nor with anything else.

Salts – boarded-up, sea-lashed, ship-empty, harbour-silted, and one bright light. Why take away the only thing we had left?

'Progress,' said Miss Pinch. 'We are not removing the light. We are removing Mr Pew. That is quite different.'

'He is the light.'

'Don't be silly.'

I saw Pew raise his head, listening to me.

'One day the ships will have no crew, and the aeroplanes will have no pilots, and the factories will be run by robots, and computers will answer the telephone, and what will happen to the people?'

'If ships had had no crew when your father came to call, your mother would have not have been a disgrace.'

'And I would not have been born.'

'You would not have been an orphan.'

'If I hadn't been an orphan, I would never have known Pew.'

'What possible difference could that have made?'

'The difference that love makes.'

Miss Pinch said nothing. She got up from the one comfortable chair where she always sat when she visited us, and swept down the spiral stairs like a hailstorm. Pew looked up, as he heard her leave – metal-capped heels, keys jangling, ferrule of her umbrella drilling every step of the stone, until she was gone in a shatter of slamming doors, and clatter of bicycle across the jetty.

'You've offended her,' said Pew.

'I offended her by being born.'

'Well, and that can't be held as your fault. It's no child's fault to be born.'

'Is it a misfortune?'

'Don't regret your life, child. It will pass soon enough.'

Pew got up and went to tend the light. When the men with computers came to automate it, it would flash every four seconds as it always did, but there would be no one to tend it, and no stories to tell. When the ships came past, no one would be saying, 'Old Pew's in there, lying his head off with his stories.'

Take the life away and only the shell is left.

I went down to my eight-legged bed. Every time I had grown, we had just stuck an extension on the bed I had, so four legs had become six, and lately, six had become eight. My dog still had his original number.

I lay there, stretched out, looking at the one star visible through the tiny window of the room. *Only connect.* How can you do that when the connections are broken?

'That's your job,' Pew had said. 'These lights connect the whole world.'

Tell me a story, Pew.

What story, child?
One that begins again.
That's the story of life.
But is it the story of my life?
Only if you tell it.

A PLACE BEFORE
THE FLOOD

Dark was walking his dog along the cliff path

when the dog sheared off in a plunging of fur and loud barking. He shouted to the dog, but the dog had a seagull in his sights. The man was angry. He was trying to concentrate on the problem in his mind: his Sunday sermon for Pentecost.

Suddenly the dog disappeared, and he heard it yelping in the distance. He sensed that something was wrong, and ran along the headland, his boots crushing the stone.

The dog had fallen over the cliff onto a ledge about twenty feet down. It was whining piteously, and holding up its paw, The man looked; there seemed to be no way down, but to fall. He couldn't climb down, and he couldn't pull the dog up.

He told the dog to stay – it could hardly do anything else, but the command gave the chaos a kind of order. It told the dog that his master was still in charge. It helped the man to believe he was still in charge.

'Stay!' he shouted. 'Lie down!' Whimpering a little, with its hurt foot, the dog did as he was told, and the man began to walk quickly back to the Manse to fetch a rope.

There was no one about at home. His wife was out. His son was at school. The cook was sleeping before the Bishop came to dinner. He was glad there was no need to explain, no need to get exasperated. A problem shared was a problem doubled, he thought. People tried to help, but all they did was interfere. Better to keep trouble contained, like a mad dog. Then he remembered his dog, and pushed aside other, more difficult thoughts. They were his thoughts. He wouldn't tell anyone, ever. He would keep his secret to himself.

He found the rope in the cart-shed. He slung it over his shoulder. He threw a heavy metal spike and a mallet into a sack, and took a pony harness to lift the dog. Then he went back, keeping his mind resolutely on the task ahead, and refusing the fraying at the edges that had become so common a mental state for him. He often felt that his mind was unravelling. Only by the greatest discipline could he find for himself the easy peace he used to take for granted. Peace of mind – he would give anything to find it again. Now he worked for it, the way he worked his body by boxing.

The man walked briskly, trying not to tread on the poppies that grew out of every crack with a bit of soil in it. He could never get them to grow in his garden, but here they grew on nothing. He might use that for his sermon …

Pentecost. He loved the story of the Grail coming to the Court of King Arthur at the Feast of Pentecost. He loved it, and it made him sad, because that day every knight had pledged to find the Grail again, and most lost their way, and even the best were destroyed. The Court was broken. Civilisation was ruined. And why? For a dream-vision that had no use in the world of men.

The story pressed in on him.

He reached the cliff face and looked down for his dog. There he was, nose between his paws, every hair a dejection. The man called to him, and the dog suddenly raised his head, eyes full of hope. The man was his god. The man wished that he too could lie and wait so patiently for salvation. 'But it will never come,' he said out loud, and then fearful of what he had said he began to bang the iron spike two-thirds of its length into the ground.

When he was sure it would take his weight, he carefully tied the rope into a reef knot, hung the horse gear across his body, and began to abseil down the cliff onto the ledge. He looked sadly at his scuffed boots; they were new last week and he had been breaking them in. His wife would scold him for the expense and risk. Life was nothing but expense and risk, he thought, with some dim hope of comfort, though it was the comfort he stressed to his flock, only himself he kept up late at night, with other thoughts.

He swung onto the ledge and patted the dog roughly and examined the injured foot. No blood, most probably a sprain, and he bound it tight, while his dog watched him with deep brown eyes.

'Come on, Tristan. Let's get you home.'

Suddenly he noticed that the wall of the cliff had a long narrow opening in it, and the edges of the opening seemed shiny, with malachite perhaps, or iron ore, polished by the salty winds. The man stepped forward, running his fingers over the bumpy edges, then he pushed himself half inside the gap, and what he saw confounded him.

The wall of the cave was made entirely of fossils. He

traced out ferns and seahorses. He found the curled-up imprint of small unknown creatures. Suddenly everything was very still; he felt that he had disturbed some presence, arrived at a moment not for him.

He looked round nervously. There was no one there, of course, but as his hands slid over the shiny brittle surface, he couldn't help pausing. He looked at the dark sea-stained wall, but how could the sea have reached here? Not since the Flood. He knew the earth was 4,000 years old, according to the Bible.

He pressed the tips of his fingers into the tight curl of the fossils, feeling them like the inside of an ear, or the inside of ... no, he wouldn't think about that. He pulled his mind away, but still his fingers moved over the raised soft edges of this mosaic of shapes. He put his fingers to his mouth, tasted sea and salt. He tasted the tang of time.

Then, for no reason at all, he felt lonely.

Dark took out his penknife and chipped away at part of the wall. He dug out an ancient seahorse, put it in his pocket, and went back to his dog.

'Steady, Tristan,' he said, securing the dog in the harness. When the dog was firm, he attached the rope to the D-ring in the middle of the gear, and quickly pulled himself back up the cliff. Then he lay down flat on his stomach, and began to haul up his dog, until he could grab it by the scruff of the neck. And help it scrabble over the edge.

They were both panting and exhausted and the man had forgotten water.

He rolled over onto his back, watching the clouds speeding over the sky, and fingering the seahorse in his pocket. He would send it to the Archaeological Society, and tell them about his find. But as he made this plan, he realised that he wanted to keep the seahorse. More than anything, he wanted to keep it, and so to the great surprise of his dog he let himself down the rope again, and gouged out another piece of eloquent rock. They were like the tablets of stone given to Moses in the desert. They were God's history and the world's. They were his inviolable law; the creation of the world, saved in stone.

When he got home he felt better, lighter, and he enjoyed his dinner with the Bishop, and later, in his study, he wrapped up the second fossil and sent it by the stable boy to the Archaeological Society. He tied a cardboard parcel label to it, with the date and place of the find.

Salts had never known anything like it. Within two weeks, scores of palaeontologists were boarding at The

Rock and Pit, spilling over into the spare rooms of spinster aunts, sleeping makeshift on camp beds at the Manse, and drawing lots for a bad night in a tent on the cliff edge.

Darwin himself came to examine the cave. He admitted to being embarrassed by the lack of fossil evidence to support some of his theories. Opponents of his *Origin of Species* wanted to know why some species seemed not to have evolved at all. Where was the so-called 'fossil-ladder'?

'The Cambrian era is very unsatisfactory,' he told his colleagues.

The cave seemed to suggest all kinds of new poss-ibilities. It was stocked like a larder with trilobites, ammonites, wavy-shelled oysters, brachiopods, brittle stars on long stalks, and although it seemed that all of these things could only have been deposited there by some terrible flood of the Noah-kind, the man with the seahorse in his pocket was unhappy.

He spent a lot of time listening to the excited voices talking about the beginning of the world. He had always believed in a stable-state system, made by God, and left alone afterwards. That things might be endlessly moving and shifting was not his wish. He didn't want a broken world. He wanted something splendid and glorious and constant.

Darwin tried to console him. 'It is not less wonderful or beautiful or grand, this world you blame on me. Only, it is less comfortable.'

Dark shrugged. Why would God make a world so imperfect that it must be continually righting itself?

It made him feel seasick. He made himself feel seasick, listing violently from one side to another, knowing that the fight in him was all about keeping control, when his hands were bloodless with gripping so tight.

If the movement in him was like the movement in the world, then how would he ever steady himself? There had to be a stable point somewhere. He had always clung to the unchanging nature of God, and the solid reliability of God's creation. Now he was faced with a maverick God who had made a world for the fun of seeing how it might develop. Had he made Man in the same way?

Perhaps there was no God at all. He laughed out loud. Perhaps, as he had always suspected, he felt lonely because he was alone.

He remembered his fingers in the hollow spirals of the fossils. He remembered his fingers in her body. No, he must not remember that, not ever. He clenched his fists.

God or no God, there seemed to be nothing to hold onto.

He felt the seahorse in his pocket.

He got it out, turned it over and over. He thought of the poor male seahorse carrying his babies in his pouch before the rising water had fastened him to the rock forever.

Fastened to the rock. He liked that hymn. *Will your anchor hold in the storms of life?* He sang it to himself: *We have an anchor that keeps the soul steadfast and sure while the billows roll. Fastened to the rock which cannot move, grounded firm and deep in the Saviour's love.*

Fastened to the rock. And he thought of Prometheus, chained to his rock for stealing fire from the gods. Prometheus, whose day-time torment was to suffer his liver torn out by an eagle, and whose night-time torment was to feel it grow back again, the skin as new and delicate as a child's.

Fastened to the rock. That was the town crest here at Salts; a sea village, a fishing village, where every wife and sailor had to believe that the unpredictable waves could be calmed by a dependable god.

Suppose the unpredictable wave was God?

The man had taken off his boots and folded his clothes neatly on top of them. He was naked and he wanted to walk slowly out to sea and never come back. There was only one thing he would take with him, and that was the seahorse. They would both swim back through time, to a place before the flood.

It was our last day as ourselves.

I had woken early to cook the bacon. While it was sizzling, I took Pew his mug of Full Strength Samson, singing to him as I went, *Will your anchor hold in the storms of life?*

'Pew! Pew!'

But he was already up and away, and he had taken DogJim with him.

I looked for him all over the lighthouse, and then I saw that the mackerel boat had gone, and the sea chest. He must have been polishing the brass first thing, because the *Brasso* and the cloths were still out, and the place gleamed, and smelled of hard work.

I ran upstairs to the light, where we kept our telescope, to identify the ships that didn't radio in. I thought I might see Pew in his boat, far out at sea. There was nobody there. The sea was empty.

It was 7 o'clock in the morning and at noon they were coming for the light. Best to leave it now, as I had always known it, and fasten it in memory, where it couldn't be destroyed. Why would I want to see them dismantling the equipment and roping off our quarters? I started to pack my own things, though there were not many, and then, in the kitchen, I saw the tin box.

I knew that Pew had left it for me, because he had put a silver coin on the top. He couldn't see to read or write, but he knew things by their shapes. My shape was a silver coin.

Pew had kept loose tea and loose tobacco in this chest. The tea and tobacco were still there, in paper bags, and underneath the bags were bundles of notes, Pew's life savings, it seemed. Underneath those were older coins, sovereigns and guineas and silver sixpences, and green threepenny bits. As well as the money, there was an old-fashioned spyglass that folded into a leather case, and a number of leather-bound books.

I took them out. Two first editions: Charles Darwin, *On the Origin of Species*, 1859, and *The Strange Case of Dr Jekyll and Mr Hyde*, 1886. The other books were the notebooks and letters that had belonged to Babel Dark.

One set of neat bound leather books was written in tiny handwriting and illustrated with ink drawings of flowers and fossils – Dark's diary of his life in Salts.

Wrapped in paper was a scuffed leather folder, with BD embossed in one corner. I undid the brown ribbon, and an untidy pile of papers scattered over my feet. The writing was big and uncertain. There were drawings of himself, always with the eyes scored out, and there were watercolours on cartridge paper of a beautiful woman, always half-turned.

I wanted to read everything, but there was no time left for me here.

Well then, this past would have to be dragged into the future, because the present had buckled under me, like a badly made chair.

The wind-once-a-week clock was still ticking, but I had to go now.

I unfolded a map of Bristol that had belonged to Josiah Dark in 1828. It was rum-stained where he had used it as a mat. On the waterfront was an inn called Ends Meet.

Perhaps Pew had gone there.

A place before the Flood.

Was there ever such a place? The Bible story is simple; God destroyed the wicked world and only Noah and his family were saved. After forty days and forty nights the ark came to rest on Mount Ararat, and as the flood waters began to subside, it stayed there.

Imagine it; evidence of an impossible moment. Marooned like a memory point above time. The thing couldn't have happened, but it did – look, there's the ship, absurd, grandiloquent, part miracle, part madness.

It's better if I think of my life like that – part miracle, part madness. It's better if I accept that I can't control any of the things that matter. My life is a trail of shipwrecks and set-sails. There are no arrivals, no destinations; there are only sandbanks and shipwreck; then another boat, another tide.

Tell me a story, Silver.

What story?
The story of what happened next.
That depends.
On what?
On how I tell it.

NEW PLANET

This is not a love story, but love is in it. That is, love is just outside it, looking for a way to break in.

We're here, there, not here, not there, swirling like specks of dust, claiming for ourselves the rights of the universe. Being important, being nothing, being caught in lives of our own making that we never wanted. Breaking out, trying again, wondering why the past comes with us, wondering how to talk about the past at all.

There's a booth in Grand Central Station where you can go and record your life. You talk. It tapes. It's the modern-day confessional – no priest, just your voice in the silence. What you were, digitally saved for the future.

Forty minutes is yours.

So what would you say in those forty minutes – what would be your death-bed decisions? What of your life will sink under the waves, and what will be like the lighthouse, calling you home?

We're told not to privilege one story above another. All the stories must be told. Well, maybe that's true, maybe all stories are worth hearing, but not all stories are worth telling.

When I look back across the span of water I call my life, I can see me there in the lighthouse with Pew, or in The Rock and Pit, or on a cliff edge finding fossils that turned out to be other lives. My life. His life. Pew. Babel Dark. All of us bound together, tidal, moon-drawn, past, present and future in the break of a wave.

There I am, edging along the rim of growing up, then the wind came and blew me away, and it was too late to shout for Pew, because he had been blown away too. I would have to grow up on my own.

And I did, and the stories I want to tell you will light up part of my life, and leave the rest in darkness. You don't need to know everything. There is no everything. The stories themselves make the meaning.

The continuous narrative of existence is a lie. There is no continuous narrative, there are lit-up moments, and the rest is dark.

When you look closely, the twenty-four hour day is framed into a moment; the still-life of the jerky amphetamine world. That woman – a pietà. Those men, rough angels with an unknown message. The children holding hands, spanning time. And in every still-life, there is a story, the story that tells you everything you need to know.

There it is; the light across the water. Your story. Mine. His. It has to be seen to be believed. And it has to be heard. In the endless babble of narrative, in spite of the daily noise, the story waits to be heard.

Some people say that the best stories have no words. They weren't brought up to Lighthousekeeping. It is true that words drop away, and that the important things are often left unsaid. The important things are learned in faces, in gestures, not in our locked tongues. The true things are too big or too small, or in any case always the wrong size to fit the template called language.

I know that. But I know something else too, because I was brought up to Lighthousekeeping. Turn down the daily noise and at first there is the relief of silence. And then, very quietly, as quiet as light, meaning returns. Words are the part of silence that can be spoken.

Dodging lorries the size of battleships, I found that the waterside tavern Ends Meet had been replaced by something called The Holiday Inn. In Pew's stories, any ordinary seaman always asked for a hammock, that being half the price of a bed, but there were no hammocks to be had at The Holiday Inn, so reluctantly I agreed to a single room and a single bed.

When I enquired about Pew, the receptionist told me they had no guest by the name of Mr Pew, but that an unusual man – that was her word, unusual, had arrived with a small dog and asked for a room. She had been unable to accommodate him, a) because the hotel had no facilities for animals, and b) because doubloons were no longer legal tender in the Eurozone.

'Where did he go?' I asked, eager and excited.

She did not know, but I felt sure he would come back for me one day.

I decided to follow Miss Pinch's advice and get a job. I would keep Pew's money until he needed it.

The next morning, scrubbed and dressed, I stood in front of the mirror in my room and wondered whether or not to wear my oilskin coat. It was yellow and oversized. And while I had never thought about it at all in the lighthouse, somehow The Holiday Inn was making me self-conscious. Bristol was supposed to be a sea-faring town, according to Pew, but yesterday I had been the only person in the shopping mall wearing a yellow oilskin.

I put on an extra jersey instead.

At the library, I presented myself, eager and willing, but the librarian told me that I had no experience and no degree.

'Can't I just put the books on the shelf for you?'

'That is not what we do.'

I looked round. The shelves were full of books.

'Well, it's what someone has to do. I'll do it for you.'

'There are no employment opportunities available at the present time.'

'I don't want an employment opportunity' (I remembered what Miss Pinch said about not being too ambitious for a Female). 'I just want a job.'

'I am afraid that won't be possible. But you may join the library if books interest you.'

'Yes, they do very much, thank you, I will.'

'Here is the form. We'll need a permanent address, utility bill, and a signed photo.'

'What, like a film star?'

'Someone who has known you for two years must sign the photo.'

'I suppose Miss Pinch might do it …' (I was beginning to wonder if this librarian was related to Miss Pinch.)

'Where do you live?'

'The Holiday Inn.'

'That is not a permanent address.'

'No, I've only just arrived here from Scotland.'

'Were you a member of the library there?'

'There was no library. We had a van came round once every three months but it only stocked Mills & Boon, True Crime, Ornithology, Second World War, Local History, which we all knew anyway because there's not that much of it, and tinned fruit. It was a bit of a grocer's too.'

'Have you proof of your address in Scotland?'

'Everyone knows it. It's the lighthouse at Cape Wrath. Straight up the coast and you can't miss it.'

'Your family are lighthousekeepers, are they?'

'No, my mother's dead, I never had a father, and Pew brought me up in the lighthouse.'

'Then, Mr Pew perhaps – he could write a letter on your behalf.'

'He's blind and I don't know where he is.'

'Take this form and return it in person to me when you have completed it.'

'Can't I join now?'

'No.'

'Can I have a job just on Saturdays?'

'No.'

'Well, I'll just come in every day and read the books then.'

And that is what I did.

The Holiday Inn was delighted to let me keep my small windowless room in return for a night-shift serving chips and peas to guests too tired to sleep. When I finished work at 5 o'clock in the morning, I slept until 11 am, and then went straight to the Public Library Reading Room.

My difficulty was that as I was not able to borrow books, I never got to the end of a story before another person took the book out on loan. I was so worried about this that I began to buy myself shiny silver note-books with laminated covers, like astronaut gear. I copied the stories out as fast as I could, but all I had so far were endless beginnings.

I had been reading *Death in Venice*, and the library was closing, so with the utmost reluctance I gave it back at the desk, and told them I would be in on the stroke of nine, first thing in the morning.

I was so tormented that someone might borrow the book before me that in the early hours of the morning I stopped serving chips and peas to the desperate, tore off my apron, and ran to the library steps like a pilgrim seeking a miracle at a shrine.

I was not the only person there.

An old drunk was crouched in a corner with a light-up model of the Eiffel Tower wired to a battery. He told me he had been happy in Paris, but he couldn't remember if it was Texas or France.

'We've all been happy once, haven't we? But why aren't we happy now? Can you tell me that?'

I couldn't.

'Y'see him there?' he said, waving vodkerishly at a swaying figure on the street. 'He goes everywhere with a dog's jacket, he does. He's just waiting for the right dog.'

'I've got a dog. His name's DogJim. He lives up in Scotland in a lighthouse.' (That had been true for most of his life though it wasn't true now.)

'Is he a Scottie dog, is he?'

'No, but he lives in Scotland.'

'Then he should be a Scottie dog – that's another thing that's wrong with life. Everything in life is wrong.'

'That's what Miss Pinch says. She says life is a torment descending into nightfall.'

'Is she a single lady?'

'Oh yes. Since she was born.'

'What's her corner?'

'I don't understand.'

'Where does she sit at night? I sit here. Where does she sit?'

'A place called Salts, in Scotland. She lives on Railing Row.'

'I might try and get up there for the summer.'

'That's the best time. In the warm.'

'What wouldn't you give to be warm? That's why I have this light-up model y'know. It warms my hands. D'y'want to warm your hands? What's a young girl like you out here for anyhow?'

'I'm waiting for the library to open.'

'You what?'

'There's a book I want to borrow – oh, it's a long story.'

(But a very short book.)

When the double doors opened, I presented myself at the desk, and asked for the book, only to discover that the librarian herself had taken it home the previous night, and this morning she had called in sick.

'Can you tell me what's the matter with her? How sick? Sick like tummy upset or a bad cold, or is it compassionate leave for a year?'

Her colleague regretted that she couldn't say – actually she couldn't care less – just went back to alphabetising a row of Sea Stories.

My stomach lurching, I left the library, and wandered about like a thing possessed. Then I found the book in a bookshop, but after I had read just one more page, the assistant came over and told me I had to buy it or leave it.

I had promised myself that I would not buy anything, except the food I needed, until I discovered the where-abouts of Pew. So I said to the assistant, 'I can't afford to buy it and I can't bear to leave it. But I love it.'

She was unmoved. We live in a world of buy it or leave it. Love does not signify.

Two days later, I was walking through the town, when I saw the librarian in Starbucks. She was sitting in the window reading *Death in Venice*. Imagine how I felt … I stood outside the window, watching her, and she kept glancing out with a faraway look, seeing only the Lido, with her nose against the heavy, plague-scented air.

A man with a dog must have thought I was a beggar, because he suddenly gave me a quid, and I went in and bought an espresso, and sat really close to her, just behind her, so that I could read the page. She must have thought I was a bit strange – I understand that because some people are a bit strange – I've met them in the hotel – but suddenly she snapped the book shut, like breaking a promise, and walked out.

I followed her.

She went to the hairdresser's, Woolworth's, the

chiropractic clinic, the pet shop, the video store, and finally back home. I lurked around until she settled down with a dish of microwave rigatoni pomadori, and *Death in Venice*.

It was agony.

At last she fell asleep, and the book slipped from her hand onto the floor.

There it was, inches away. If only I could lift up the window and drag it towards me. The book was half-closed where it lay on the blue carpet. I tried to coax it with magnetic powers. I said, 'Come on, this way!'

The book didn't move. I tried lifting the window, but it was locked. I felt like Lancelot outside the Chapel of the Grail – but I've never finished that story either.

Days passed. I kept an eye on her until she got better. I did more than that; I pushed aspirins through the letterbox. I would have donated to the blood bank if it had been a help, but she got better, with or without me, and the day came when I followed her back to the library.

She took the book inside, checked it, and went to deal with a customer. I grabbed the book from the white plastic wheelie cart they use to trolley the books back to the shelves. Just as I was heading for the Reading Room, an assistant with a moustache – she was a woman but she had a moustache, which is usually a bad sign – this assistant pulled the book from my hands, and said it was reserved for a customer.

'I'm a customer,' I said

'Name?' she said, as though it were a crime.

'I'm not on your list.'

'Then you will have to wait until the book is returned again,' she said, with evident satisfaction, and that's the thing about some librarians – they love telling you a book is out of print, borrowed, lost, or not even written yet.

I have a list of titles that I leave at the desk, because they are bound to be written some day, and it's best to be ahead of the queue.

That evening I followed the librarian home, because I had got used to following her home, and habit is hard to break. She went in, as usual, and when she came back out to sit in the garden, she was carrying her Own Copy of *Death In Venice*. All I had to do was to wait for the phone to ring, which it did, and then I ran across the front lawn, and grabbed the book.

Suddenly I heard her screaming into the phone, 'There's an intruder – yes, it's the same one – get the police!'

I rushed to help her, but she wouldn't stop scream-

144

ing, so I searched all over the house, and I couldn't find anybody, which is what I told the police when they arrived. They took no notice, just arrested me, because she said I was the intruder – when all I had wanted was to borrow her book.

After that, things got tougher, because the police discovered that as I had no mother or father, I didn't officially exist. I asked them to telephone Miss Pinch, but she claimed never to have heard of such a person as myself.

The police had me interviewed by a nice man who turned out to be a psychiatrist for Young Offenders, although I hadn't offended anyone except for the librarian and Miss Pinch. I explained about *Death in Venice*, and the problems I had had joining the library, and the psychiatrist nodded and suggested I come in once a week for observation, like I was a new planet.

Which, in a way, I was.

Dark was looking at the moon.

If the earth's history was fossil-written, why not the universe? The moon, bone-white, bleached of life, was the relic of a solar system once planeted with Earths.

He thought the whole of the sky must have been alive once, and some stupidity or carelessness had brought it to this burnt-out, warmless place.

When he was a boy he used to imagine the sky as the sea and the stars as ships lit up at the mast. At night, when the sea was black, and the sky was black, the stars ploughed the surface of the water, furrowing it like a ship's keel. He had amused himself by lobbing stones at the star's reflections, hitting them and bursting them, watching them steady and return.

Now the sky was a dead sea, and the stars and the planets were memory-points, like Darwin's fossils. There were archives of catastrophe and mistake. Dark wished that there was nothing there at all; no evidence, no way of knowing. What Darwin called knowledge and progress, Dark understood as a baleful diary; a book that had been better left unread. There was so much in life that had been better left unread.

It is good to wander along the sea-coast, when formed of moderately hard rocks, and watch the process of degradation. The tides, in most cases, reach the cliffs for only a short time twice a day, and the waves eat into them only when they are charged with sand or pebbles; for there is reason to believe that pure water can effect little or nothing in wearing away a rock. At last, the base of the cliff is undermined, huge fragments fall down, and these remaining fixed, have to be worn away, atom by atom, until reduced in size, until they can be rolled about the waves, and then are more quickly ground into pebbles, sand or mud.

Dark put the book aside. He had read it so many times, and seen in himself all the marks of gradual erosion. Well, perhaps he would be found later, unrecognisable but for his teeth – yes, his stubborn jaw would be the last thing to go. Words, all words, scattered by the waves.

I sometimes think of myself, up at Am Parbh.

The Turning Point, knowing I was going to leave. *Going to leave, would have to leave,* subtle changes in inflection, denoting different states of mind, but with the same end in view, except that there is no end, and when it is in view, it is always a sighted ship that will never come to shore.

Still, the ship must be sighted, we must pack for the sailing. We have to believe in our control, in our future. But when the future does come it comes like the *McCloud*, fully equipped with the latest technology and a new crew, but with the old *McCloud* riding inside.

The fossil record is always there, whether or not you discover it. The brittle ghosts of the past. Memory is not like the surface of the water – either troubled or still.

Memory is layered. What you were was another life, but the evidence is somewhere in the rock – your trilobites and ammonites, your struggling life-forms, just when you thought you could stand upright.

Years ago in Railings Row, on two kitchen chairs pushed together, under Miss Pinch's One Duck Eiderdown, I cried for a world that could be stable and sure. I didn't want to start again. I was too small and too tired.

Pew taught me that nothing is gone, that everything can be recovered, not as it was, but in its changing form.

'Nothing keeps the same form forever, child, not even Pew.'

Before he wrote *On the Origin of Species*, Darwin spent five years as a naturalist, aboard HMS *Beagle*. In nature, he found not past, present and future as we recognise them, but an evolutionary process of change – energy never trapped for too long – life always becoming.

When Pew and I were spun out of the lighthouse like beams and sparks, I wanted everything to continue as it had. I wanted something solid and trustworthy. Twice-flung – first from my mother, and then Pew – I looked for a safe landing and soon made the mistake of finding one.

But the only thing to do was to tell the story again.

Tell me a story, Silver.

What story?

The story of the talking bird.

That was later, much later, when I had landed and grown up.

It's still your story.

Yes.

TALKING BIRD

Two facts about Silver:
It reflects 95% of its own light. It is
one of the few precious metals that
can be safely eaten in small quantities.

I had gone to Capri, because I feel better surrounded
by water.

As I was winding down one of the whitewashed alleys
on the hillside overlooking the Grotto Azzurro, I heard
someone calling my name – 'Bongiorno, Silver!'

In the window of a small apartment was a big cage,
and in the big cage was a beady beaky bird.

I know it was a coincidence – even though Jung says
there is no such thing, I know it wasn't magic – just a
trained voice-box with feathers, but it matched a
moment in me that was waiting for someone to call my
name. Names are still magic; even Sharon, Karen,

Darren and Warren are magic to somebody somewhere. In the fairy stories, naming is knowledge. When I know your name, I can call your name, and when I call your name, you'll come to me.

So the bird called, 'Bongiorno, Silver!' and I stood and looked at him for a long time, until the woman inside thought I was a thief or a madman, and banged on the window with a little statue of the Madonna.

I motioned for her to come outside, and I asked her if I could buy the bird.

'No no no!' she said, 'Quell'uccello è mia vita!' (*'That bird is my life!'*)

'What, your whole life?'

'Si si si! Mio marito è morte, mio figlio sta nell'esercito e ho soltano un rene.' (*'My husband is dead, my son is in the army, I have only one kidney.'*)

This was not looking good for either of us. She clutched the Madonna.

'Se non fosse per quell'uccello e il mio abbonamento alla *National Geographic Magazine* non avrei niente.' (*'And without that bird and my subscription to* National Geographic Magazine, *I would have nothing.'*)

'Nothing?'

'Niente! Rien! Zilch!'

She slammed the door and put the statue of the Madonna in the birdcage in the window. Wingless and grounded, I slunk off for an espresso.

Such a beautiful island – blue, cream, pink, orange. But I was colour-blind that day. I wanted that bird.

That night, I crept back to the apartment and looked in through the window. The woman was lolling asleep in the chair watching *Batman* dubbed into Italian.

I walked round to her door and tried the handle. It was open! I let myself in and crept forward into the little room full of hand-crocheted lace and plastic flowers. The bird regarded me – 'Pretty boy! Pretty boy!' Who cares about gender at a time like this?

On tiptoe, ridiculous and serious, I went to the cage, unlatched the wire door, and seized the bird. He jumped onto my finger quite happily, but the woman was stirring, and then the bird began to sing something dreadful about going back to Sorrento.

Quick as a dart, I slid a lace doily over his beak, and slipped out of the room and into the alley.

I was a thief. I had stolen the bird.

For six months I lived nervously on my part of the island, refusing to go home because I couldn't put the bird in quarantine. My partner came out to visit me and asked me why I wouldn't come home. I said I couldn't come home – it was a question of the bird.

'Your business is failing and your relationship is failing – forget the bird.'

Forget the bird! I might as well try and forget myself. And that was the problem of course – I had forgotten myself, long since, long before the bird, and I wanted, in a messy, maddening way, to go on forgetting myself and yet, to find myself too. When the bird said my name it was as though I had just heard it, not for the first time, but after a long time, like somebody coming out of a drugged dream.

'Bongiorno, Silver!' Every day the bird reminded me of my name, which is to say, who I am.

I wish I could be clearer. I wish I could say, 'My life had no light. My life was eating me alive.' I wish I could say, 'I was having a mental breakdown, so I stole a bird.' Strictly speaking that would be true, and it is why the police let me go, instead of charging me with the theft of a much-beloved macaw. The Italian doctor put me on Prozac and sent me for a series of appointments at the Tavistock Clinic in London. The woman whose bird it had been, and was again, felt sorry for me; after all, she might have lost a parrot but she was not cuckoo. She gave me a pile of old *National Geographic* magazines to read in the loony bin, which is where the nice man at the pizza place told her I would be spending the rest of my life.

The rest of my life. I have never rested, always run, run so fast that the sun can't make a shadow. Well, here I am – mid-way, lost in a dark wood – this selva oscura, without a torch, a guide, or even a bird.

The psychiatrist was a gentle, intelligent man with very clean fingernails. He asked me why I had not sought help sooner.

'I don't need help – not this kind anyway. I can dress myself, make toast, make love, make money, make sense.'

'Why did you steal the bird?'

'I love the stories of Talking Birds, especially Siegfried, who is led out of the forest and into the treasure by the Woodbird. Siegfried is stupid enough to listen to birds, and I thought that the peck, peck, pecking at the pane of my life might mean that I should listen too.'

'You thought the bird was talking to you?'

'Yes, I know the bird was talking to me.'

'Was there no human being you could have talked to instead?'

'I wasn't talking to the bird. The bird was talking to me.'

There was a long pause. There are some things that shouldn't be said in company. See above.

I tried to put right the damage.

'I went to a therapist once, and she gave me a copy of a book called *The Web Not Woven*. Frankly, I would rather listen to the bird.'

Now I had made things much worse for myself.

'Would you like another bird?'

'It wasn't any old bird; it was a bird that knew my name.'

The doctor leaned back in his chair. 'Do you keep a diary?'

'I have a collection of silver notebooks.'

'Are they consistent?'

'Yes. I buy them from the same department store.'

'I mean, do you keep one record of your life, or several? Do you feel you have more than one life perhaps?'

'Of course I do. It would be impossible to tell one single story.'

'Perhaps you should try.'

'A beginning, a middle, and an end?'

'Something like that – yes.'

I thought of Babel Dark and his neat brown note-books, and his wild torn folder. I thought of Pew tearing stories out of light.

'Do you know the story of Jekyll and Hyde?'

'Of course.'

'Well then – to avoid either extreme, it is necessary to find all the lives in between.'

The seahorse was in his pocket.

Dark was walking along the beach.

The moon was new, and laid on her back, as though she had been blown over by the wind that gusted the sand round his boots.

He looked out towards Cape Wrath, and thought he saw the figure of Pew in the glass of the light. The waves were fierce and rapid. There was going to be a storm.

1878. His fiftieth birthday.

When Robert Louis Stevenson had asked if he might visit him, Dark had been pleased. They would go to the lighthouse, and then Dark would show him the famous fossil cave. He knew that Stevenson was fascinated by Darwin's theories of evolution. He had no idea that Stevenson had a particular purpose to his visit.

The men had sat on either side of the fire talking. They had both drunk a good deal of wine, and Stevenson was flushed and animated. Did not Dark think that all men had atavistic qualities? Parts of themselves that lay like undeveloped negatives? Shadow selves, unpictured but present?

Dark felt his breathing shorten. His heart was beating. What did Stevenson mean?

'A man might be two men,' said Stevenson, 'and not know it, or he might discover it and find that he had to act on it. And those two men would be of very different kinds. One upright and loyal, the other, perhaps not much better than an ape.'

'I do not accept that men were once apes,' said Dark.

'But you accept that all men have ancestors. What's to say that somewhere in your blood there isn't a long-gone fiend that only lacks a body?'

'In *my* blood?'

'Or mine. Any one of us. When we talk about a man acting out of character, what are we honestly saying? Aren't we saying that there must be more to the man than we choose to know, or indeed more than he chooses to know about himself?'

'Are we so utterly lacking in self-knowledge, do you think?'

'I wouldn't put it like that, Dark; a man may know himself, but he prides himself on his character, his integrity – the word says it all – *integrity* – we use it to mean virtue, but it means wholeness too, and which of us is that?'

'We are all whole, I hope.'

'Do you wilfully misunderstand me, I wonder?'

'What do you mean by that?' said Dark, and his mouth was dry and Stevenson noticed how he played with his watch chain like a rosary.

'Shall I be frank?'

'Please do.'

'I was in Bristol ...'

'I see.'

'And I met a sailor by the name of – '

'Price,' said Dark.

He got up and went to look out of the window, and when he turned back into his study, full of well-worn and familiar things, he felt like a stranger in his own life.

'I will tell you then,' he said.

He was talking, telling the whole story from beginning to end, but he heard his voice far off, like a man in another room. He was overhearing himself. It was himself he was talking to. Himself he needed to tell.

If I had not seen her again that day in London, perhaps my life would have been very different. I waited a month for our next meeting and I thought of nothing else that month. As soon as we were together, she turned round and asked me to unhook her dress. There were twenty hooks; I remember counting them.

She stepped out of her dress and uncoiled her hair and kissed me. She was so free with her body. Her body, her freedom. I was afraid of how she made me feel. You say we are not one, you say truly there are two of us. Yes, there were two of us, but we were one. As for myself, I am splintered by great waves. I am coloured glass from a church window long since shattered. I find pieces of myself everywhere, and I cut myself handling them. The reds and greens of her body are the colours of my love for her, the coloured parts of me, not the thick heavy glass of the rest.

I am a glass man, but there is no light in me that can shine across the sea. I shall lead no one home, save no lives, not even my own.

She came here once. Not to this house, but to the lighthouse. That makes it bearable for me to go on living here. Every day I walk the way we walked, and I try and pick out her imprint. She trailed her hands along the sea wall. She sat by a rock with her back to the wind. She made this bleak place bountiful. Some of her is in the wind, is in the poppies, is in the dive of the gulls. I find her when I look, even though I will never see her again.

I find her in the lighthouse and its long flashes over

the water, I found her in the cave – miraculous, impossible, but she was there, the curve of her caught up in the living rock. When I put my hand in the gap, it's her I feel; her salty smoothness, her sharp edges, her turnings and openings, her memory.

Darwin said something to me once for which I was grateful. I had been trying to forget, trying to stop my mind reaching for a place where it can never home. He knew my agitation, though he did not know its cause, and he took me up to Am Parbh – the Turning Point, and with his hand on my shoulder, he said, 'Nothing can be forgotten. Nothing can be lost. The universe itself is one vast memory system. Look back and you will find the beginnings of the world.'

1859

Charles Darwin published *On the Origin of Species,* and Richard Wagner completed his opera *Tristan and Isolde.* Both are about the beginnings of the world.

Darwin – objective, scientific, empirical, quantifiable.

Wagner – subjective, poetic, intuitive, mysterious.

In *Tristan* the world shrinks to a boat, a bed, a lantern, a love-potion, a wound. The world is contained within a word – Isolde.

The Romantic solipsism that nothing exists but the two of us, could not be farther from the multiplicity and variety of Darwin's theory of the natural world. Here, the world and everything in it forms and is re-formed, tirelessly and unceasingly. Nature's vitality is amoral and unsenti-mental; the weak die, the strong survive.

Tristan, weak and wounded, should have died. Love healed him. Love is not part of natural selection.

Where did love begin? What human being looked at another and saw in their face the forests and the sea? Was there a day, exhausted and weary, dragging home food, arms cut and scarred, that you saw yellow flowers and, not knowing what you did, picked them because I love you?

In the fossil record of our existence, there is no trace of love. You cannot find it held in the earth's crust, waiting to be discovered. The long bones of our ancestors show nothing of their hearts. Their last meal is sometimes preserved in peat or in ice, but their thoughts and feelings are gone.

Darwin overturned a stable-state system of creation and completion. His new world was flux, change, trial and error, maverick shifts, chance, fateful experiments, and lottery odds against success. But earth had turned out to be the blue ball with the winning number. Bobbing alone in a sea of space, earth was the lucky number.

Darwin and his fellow scientists still had no idea how old earth and her life forms might be, but they knew they were unimaginably older than Biblical time, which dated the earth at 4,000 years. Now, time had to be understood mathematically. It could no longer be imagined as a series of lifetimes, reeled off like a genealogy from the Book of Genesis. The distances were immense.

And yet, the human body is still the measure of all things. This is the scale we know best. This ridiculous six feet belts the globe and everything in it. We talk about feet, hands, spans, because that is what we know. We know the world by and through our bodies. This is our lab; we can't experiment without it.

It is our home too. The only home we really possess. Home is where the heart is …

The simple image is complex. My heart is a muscle with four valves. It beats 101,000 times a day, it pumps eight pints of blood around my body. Science can bypass it, but I can't. I say I give it to you, but I never do.

Don't I? In the fossil record of my past, there is evidence that the heart has been removed more than once. The patient survived.

Broken limbs, drilled skulls, but no sign of the heart. Dig deeper, and there'll be a story, layered by time, but true as now.

Tell me a story, Silver.

What story?
The story of Tristan and Isolde.

SOME WOUNDS

Some wounds never heal.

The second time the sword went in, I aimed it at the place of the first.

I am weak there – the place where I had been found out before. My weakness was skinned over by your love.

I knew when you healed me that the wound would open again. I knew it like destiny, and at the same time, I knew it as choice.

The love-potion? I never drank it. Did you?

Our story is so simple. I went to bring you back for someone else, and won you for myself. Magic, they all said later, and it was, but not the kind that can be brewed.

We were in Ireland. Was there ever a country so damp? I had to wring out my mind to think clearly. I was a morning mist of confusion.

You had a lover. I killed him. It was war and your man was on the losing side. As I killed him, he fatally wounded me; that is, he gave me the wound that only love could repair. Love lost, and the wound would be as bloody as ever. As bloody as now, bed-soaked and jagged.

I didn't care about dying. But you took me in out of pity because you didn't know my name. I told you it was Tantrist, and as Tantrist you loved me.

'What if I was Tristan?' I asked you one day, and I watched you grow pale, and take a dagger. You had every right to kill me. I turned my throat to you, Adam's apple twitching slightly, but before I closed my eyes, I smiled.

When I opened them again, you had put down the dagger and you were holding my hand. I felt like a little child, not a hero, not a warrior, not a lover, only a boy in a big bed, the day turning round him, dreamy and slow.

The room was high and blue. Cobalt blue. There was an orange fire. Your eyes were green. Lost in the colours of our love I never forgot them, and now, lying here, where the sheets are brown with my blood, it is blue and orange and green I remember. A little boy in a big bed.

Where are you?

We said nothing. You sat beside me. You were the strong one. I couldn't stand up. Holding my hand, and stroking it gently with your finger and thumb, you touched in me another world. Until then, through wounds and wreck, I had been sure of myself. I was Tristan. Now, my name gone backwards, I went backwards myself, unravelling into strands of feeling. This stranded man.

When it was time for me to sail back to Cornwall, you came out and stood on a narrow rock, and we watched each other so far that only we two knew what was rock or boat or human.

The sea was empty. The sky was shut.

Then King Marke sent me to fetch you to be his wife.

You said you wanted to kill me.

Again I opened my body to you. Again you dropped the blade.

When your servant brought the drink I knew you intended to poison me. Under the cliffs of Cornwall, the King in his boat ready to meet us, I drank the water, because that's what it was. Your servant had given me water. You drank too, and fell to the floor, and I went to catch you and hold you as the men dropped anchor and the ship lurched. You were in my arms for the first time, and you said my name, 'Tristan.'

I answered you: 'Isolde.'

Isolde. The world became a word.

We lived for the night. The torch in your window was my signal. When it was lit, I stayed away. When you extinguished it, I came to you – secret doors, dark corridors, forbidden stairs, brushing aside fear and propriety like cobwebs. I was inside you. You contained me. Together, in bed, we could sleep, we could dream, and if we heard your servant's mournful cry, we called it a bird or a dog. I never wanted to wake. I had no use for the day. The light was a lie. Only here, the sun killed, and time's hands bound, were we free. Imprisoned in each other, we were free.

When my friend Melot set the trap, I think I knew it. I turned to death full face, as I had turned to love with my whole body. I would let death enter me as you had entered me. You had crept along my blood vessels through the wound, and the blood that circulates returns to the heart. You circulated me, you made me blush like a girl in the hoop of your hands. You were in my arteries and my lymph, you were the colour just under my skin, and if I cut myself, it was you I bled. Red Isolde, alive on my fingers, and always the force of blood pushing you back to my heart.

In the fight when Marke found us, I fought at the door until you escaped. Then I faced Melot at last, my friend, my trusted friend, and I held my sword at him, red with blood. As he lifted his sword against me, I threw mine down and ran his through my body, at the bottom of my ribs. The skin, still shy of healing, opened at once.

When I woke, I was here, in my own castle, across the sea, carried and guarded by my servant. He told me he had sent for you, yes surely there was a sail? I could see it swift as love. He climbed into the watchtower, but there was no sail.

I put my hand into the bloody gap at the bottom of my ribs. Her name drips through my fingers: *Isolde*. Where are you?

Tristan, I didn't drink it either. There was no love-potion, only love. It was you I drank.

Tristan, wake up. Don't die of the wound. Divide the night with me, and die together in the morning.

His eye is pale, his breathing is still. When I first saw him, he was still and pale, and I kissed him into life, though he never knew that was the art I used.

Tristan, the world was made so that we could find each other in it. Already the world is fading, returning to the sea. My pulse ebbs with yours. Death frees us from the torment of parting. I cannot part with you. I am you.

The world is nothing. Love formed it.

The world vanishes without trace.

What is left is love.

The pot of Full Strength Samson was finished.

Dark and Pew were drinking their tea in silence, as they always did. Dark broke it.

'Do you recall my visitor?'

Pew sucked on his pipe before he spoke.

'Darwin? Oh aye, I recall him, and Salts like a great cheese o'r-swarmed wi' mice.'

'I woke up in one world and I went to bed in another.'

'It was but a fancy of his, Reverend. A boy playing with shells.'

'No, not a fancy, Pew. The world is older than we can dream it. And how it came about, we hardly know.'

'You don't believe that the guid God made it in seven days then?'

'No, I do not.'

'Well, an' that is hard fir ye then.'

'Yes, hard, but not as hard as other things.'

There was another silence. Dark shifted in his chair so that he could re-tie his boots.

'Do you recall my visitor?'

There was a great puffing, like an engine, before Pew spoke.

'Stevenson? Oh aye, and he ran up and down this lighthouse without coughing once, though his lungs, they say, have more holes than a cod net.'

'He has published this book. He sent it to me today.'

Dark passed it to Pew who ran his hands over the cover, feeling the tooled leather and the engraved type. *The Strange Case of Dr Jekyll and Mr Hyde.*

'Is it aboot lighthousekeeping?'

'In a manner of speaking, it is – if keeping the light is the one thing all of us must do.'

'Oh aye, we must do it all right.'

'This story of his is about a man named Dr Henry Jekyll; an upright beacon, a shining example, a fellow of penetrating intellect and glowing humanity.

'Well then …' said Pew, re-filling his pipe, and sensing a story.

'Well then, by means of a drug he manufactures himself in his laboratory, he can transform himself at will into a stunted dark creature by the name of Edward

Hyde. A thing of infamy and villainy. But the twist is that Hyde is able to do all of the things that Jekyll secretly longs to do. The one is all virtue and the other is all vice. But while they may seem to be entirely separate, the dreadful and disturbing part, is that they are the same person. Listen to how Jekyll reasons it to himself:

If each, I told myself, could be but housed in separate identities, life would be relieved of all that was unbearable; the unjust might go his way, delivered from the aspirations and remorse of his more upright twin; and the just could walk steadfastly and securely on his upward path, doing the good things in which he found pleasure, and no longer exposed to disgrace and penitence by the hands of this extraneous evil.

Pew sucked on his pipe. 'I'd rather walk at night with a clean-bodied villain than a clean-clothed saint.'

'The crimes of this man Hyde multiply even to murder, and of course, after a time, Jekyll finds himself remaining as Hyde even when he has taken the potion to restore himself to Jekyll. Eventually Hyde takes over completely.

The hand which I now saw, clearly enough, in the yellow light of a mid-London morning, lying half shut on the bedclothes, was lean, corded, knuckly, of a dusky pallor and thickly shaded with a smart growth of hair. It was the hand of Edward Hyde.

Dark paused. 'Pew, when Stevenson came to visit me, and we sat in my study talking, he asked me if I thought a man might have two natures; the one almost ape-like and bestial in its fury, the other committed to self-improvement. Of course Darwin is much to blame for all this, with his monkey talk, though he has been misread, I know. I told Stevenson I did not believe that Man was descended from the Ape, or that he shared with such a creature a common inheritance.'

'Well spoken all right,' said Pew.

'And then, Stevenson said he had been lately in Bristol, where he had met a seaman by the name of ...'

'Price,' said Pew.

'That is correct. And I told him all there is to tell. You understand me, Pew? All there is to tell.

There was another pause – longer this time, like a difficult thought.

'Do you recall my visitor?'

Pew took his pipe from his mouth and answered at once, 'Oh aye, Mrs Tenebris.'

'Her married name was Lux. Her maiden name was O'Rourke.'

'She was a fine woman.'

'You allowed me to bring her here, and for that kindness I am bound to you.'

Pew waved his pipe.

'You understand me, Pew? I am Henry Jekyll.' He

paused for a moment, looking at his hands, strong, long, studious. 'And I am Edward Hyde.'

It was a southerly wind that blew along the headland, pushing the hair back from his face. He was fifty-eight, and his hair was still thick, but white as the bleached bones he threw to his dog in place of a stick.

The obvious equation was Dark=Jekyll. Lux=Hyde. The impossible truth was that in his life it was the reverse.

He walked on – turning it over and over in his hands, as he had done for so many years now. He took the seahorse out of his pocket – his emblem of lost time.

Stevenson had not believed him when Dark told him that all the good in his life had lived in Bristol with Molly. Only Lux was kind and human and whole. Dark was a hypocrite, an adulterer and a liar.

'But he is me,' said Dark, 'and I must live with him even though I hate him.'

Could he not now, even now, resolve his nature? Why was it too late?

He understood that when Molly had come to Salts it had been his last chance. His freedom. She had come to forgive him and to rescue him. She had wanted to take him away. She had wanted them to disappear that night on a packet boat and go to France.

Why had he not gone?

His life here was hateful to him. His two months a year with her had made it bearable. She was the air pocket in his upturned boat.

Now he had drowned.

He took out his notebook, scuffed and scored and looked at the entry.

Molly returned to Bristol. I would not accept her plan of our new life in France. I stood firm. I stood firm. I stood firm.

He closed the book and shoved it in his pocket and walked on, noticing how the cliffs were worn away at the base.

Tell me a story, Silver.

What story?
The story of how we met.

Love is an unarmed intruder.

The boat was coming into the port at Athens.

It was the last boat, and already the lights were lit. I had been waiting for an hour or so, among the backpacks and ice-cream and endless cigarettes of the others like me who had an island to reach before dark.

The boat was vacuum-packed with Albanians, four generations to a family: great-grandmother, air-dried like a chilli pepper, deep red skin and a hot temper; grandmother, all sun-dried tomato, tough, chewy, skin split with the heat; getting the kids to rub olive oil into her arms; mother, moist as a purple fig, open everywhere – blouse, skirt, mouth, eyes, a wide-open woman, lips licking the salt spray flying from the open boat. Then there were the kids, aged four and six, a couple of squirts, zesty as lemons.

I sat on my luggage, fearing it would disappear inside their warehouse-loads of boxes and sacks, string-tied. When we reached the island, their men were waiting with their mules, and the whole family jumped onto the wooden saddles and rode barefoot up the ladder-steep alleyways, towards tiered white buildings that got darker and darker as we moved away from the lit-up holiday feel of the port, its coloured lights in swags around the harbour.

Hydra: a mule-backed, four-legged island, whose only wheels belong to the municipal dustcart.

I walked out onto the spur of the harbour, avoiding excitable restaurant owners waving lobsters, and attentive barman serving Pina Coladas in jugs the size of football trophies.

I was trying to find an address.

There was a security guard standing smartly by an anchored yacht whose owners had dressed for dinner and were eating it. Well, almost eating it – the women raising empty forks to glossy famished lips, and the men the colour of beef fillet, drinking goblets of Krug. I know it was Krug; I saw the bottle shape as the waiter poured it.

He shook his head when I showed him my address – he was only in town for the night. 'You can stay with me,' he said, winking. 'I got a nice berth and I can join you about 5 am, when you've had some rest.'

I liked him. I put down my bags. He gave me a beer. We started talking.

'They're a New Zealand family,' he said. 'They're good employers. I've been all over the world. We're heading down to Capri tomorrow. Ever been to Capri?'

I began to say something about a bird, and then I thought better of it, and asked him about himself.

'Just drifting,' he said, 'if you'll excuse the pun. I'll do this for a couple of years and I might meet somebody, find a place I want to settle down – maybe run a boat business of my own – who knows – there's plenty of time.'

'Do you have to stand here all night?'

'Yep, all night.'

'What did you do before this?'

'I was married. Then I wasn't married any more. Tipped up, flung out, recognise that?'

I did.

'End of story. Gotta start again. Gotta be positive. Gotta move on. Don't look back. No regrets.'

That's how he said it. He said it like a mantra. I wonder how many times a day he had to say it to make it true? It was a poultice over his heart.

I don't know how to poultice my heart.

I thanked him for the beer, and picked up my bags.
'You sure now about that 5 am?'

I was sure. This wasn't the night for adventure. I
wanted to get to the place, rented sight unseen, from a
friend of a friend. I had the keys but no instructions –
like life really – and as I toiled on foot up and up the
steep whitewashed steps, the old Greek women sitting
outside regarded me, and sometimes greeted me with a
Kalispera.

At last, sweat pouring off me, and my bags banging
against my body, I found the heavy maroon door of my
house. I pushed myself inside, startling a tiny cat that
vanished like good luck, and in the flare of my matches
I walked across the ghost-sheen of the white floor paint,
trying to find the lights.

I couldn't find them, so I dumped my bags, lit a
candle, and pulled out the bottle of wine, and the
bread and olive oil and sausage I had brought with me.
I found a blunt knife (why are knives always blunt?) and
a plate and a glass, and went and sat wearily on the flat
roof that looked out and down towards the sea.

The night was very quiet; dogs barking and the
scissor-sound of bats cutting the air, but no human
noise, except for the television set, very faint from the

house behind, where I could see a crucifix on the wall, and an old woman putting on her nightdress.

I opened the wine. It was strong and good. I began to feel better.

The stones under my feet were warm. The old lady in the house behind came out to water her tomato plants. I could hear the hiss of the hose, and her sister talking to her from inside. Her sister had climbed into bed and was watching television and calling out the news. I could smell sardines grilling, and in the mountains the night-dogs were starting to bark – the concrete walls bouncing the woofs.

Woof, woof, woof woof, never quite sure where it's coming from. Never quite sure where the noises in the night are coming from.

After the Talking Bird, the nice man at the Tavistock Clinic kept asking me why I stole books and birds, though I had only ever stolen one of each.

I told him it was about meaning, and he suggested, very politely, that might be a kind of psychosis.

'You think meaning is psychosis?'

'An obsession with meaning, at the expense of the ordinary shape of life, might be understood as psychosis, yes.'

'I do not accept that life has an ordinary shape, or

that there is anything ordinary about life at all. We make it ordinary, but it is not.'

He twiddled his pencil. His nails were very clean.

'I am only asking questions.'

'So am I.'

There was a pause.

I said, 'How would you define psychosis?'

He wrote on a piece of paper with his pencil: *Psychosis: out of touch with reality.*

Since then, I have been trying to find out what reality is, so that I can touch it.

Sleepy with travelling and the night and the wine, I went inside and lay down on the bare pink mattress. I should have been looking for linen, but I fell asleep, thinking about Babel Dark, and what it was like to be lost and alone a hundred and fifty years ago.

I dreamed of a door, and it was opening.

In the morning I was woken early by the chromatic bell of the Orthodox Church.

I unlatched the shutters. The light was as intense as a love affair. I was blinded, delighted, not just because it was warm and wonderful, but because nature measures nothing. Nobody needs this much sunlight. Nobody needs droughts, volcanoes, monsoons, tornadoes either, but we get them, because our world is as extravagant as a world can be. We are the ones obsessed by measurement. The world just pours it out.

I went outside, tripping over slabs of sunshine the size of towns. The sun was like a crowd of people, it was a party, it was music. The sun was blaring through the walls of the houses and beating down the steps. The sun was drumming time into the stone. The sun was rhythming the day.

'Why are you afraid?' I asked myself, because fear is at the bottom of everything, even love usually rests on fear. 'Why are you afraid, when whatever you do you will die anyway?'

I decided to walk to the convent on the other side of the island.

It's a steep climb, up a winding track of scrub and vipers, unshaded from the sun.

Nobody comes up here, and if they do, they mule-ride, side-saddle, the men with luxury moustaches and the women, heads covered, arms bare.

It is here that the one and only diesel dustcart deposits its foul load. There is a Dante's Inferno of smouldering rubbish, with a stench that only humans can produce. I took off my T-shirt, wrapped it round my head, and ran till my lungs collapsed, but at least I was free of the worst of it.

Free, and climbing higher and higher, the island under me like a lover.

I felt I was being watched. The road was empty. My feet were dirty, my ankles were rimmed with dust. There was a bird of prey arcing the clouds – but nothing animal or human.

Then I saw it – about the size of a medium dog but looking like a cat, with bigger ears and frightening eyes. It was crouched on a rock outside a ruined monastery, like a John the Baptist refusing consolation.

It was a civet.

I went as close as I dared, and instead of turning tail, it threatened to spring.

We stared each other out – until it silently slunk backwards into a cave behind the rock.

I am part civet, part mouser.

What should I do about the wild and the tame? The wild heart that wants to be free, and the tame heart that wants to come home. I want to be held. *I don't want you to come too close.* I want you to scoop me up and bring me home at nights. *I don't want to tell you where I am.* I want to keep a place among the rocks where no one can find me. *I want to be with you.*

I used to be a hopeless romantic. I am still a hopeless romantic. I used to believe that love was the highest value. I still believe that love is the highest value. I don't expect to be happy. I don't imagine that I will find love, whatever that means, or that if I do find it, it will make me happy. I don't think of love as the answer or the solution. I think of love as a force of nature – as strong as the sun, as necessary, as impersonal, as gigantic, as impossible, as scorching as it is warming, as drought-making as it is life-giving. And when it burns out, the planet dies.

My little orbit of life circles love. I daren't get any closer. I'm not a mystic seeking final communion. I don't go out without SPF 15. I protect myself.

But today, when the sun is everywhere, and everything solid is nothing but its own shadow, I know that the real things in life, the things I remember, the things I turn over in my hands, are not houses, bank accounts, prizes or promotions. What I remember is love – all love – love of this dirt road, this sunrise, a day by the river, the stranger I met in a café. Myself, even, which is the hardest thing of all to love, because love and selfishness are not the same thing. It is easy to be selfish. It is hard to love who I am. No wonder I am surprised if you do.

But love it is that wins the day. On this burning road, fenced with barbed wire to keep the goats from straying, I find for a minute what I came here for, which is a sure sign that I will lose it again instantly.

I felt whole.

At the convent, I rang the bell, reading the notice to be patient.

Eventually, the door over the wooden grille opened and I saw the face of the nun. She slid back the bolts and ushered me in, speaking kindnesses I couldn't understand. She untucked a cloth from her belt and wiped a chair already spotless with dusting. I sat down and she bowed and made a mime of drinking, so I nodded and smiled, and she brought me a tray of thick coffee, thin biscuits, and rose-petal jam from her garden.

There were two cups on the tray. I thought that the nun intended to join me, but she withdrew. I took out some money and went to the chapel to make an offering. There was a woman inside, kneeling in prayer.

'I'm sorry,' I said. 'I didn't mean to intrude.'

You smiled, stood up, and came out into the sunshine. Perhaps it was the light on your face, but I thought I recognised you from somewhere a long way down, somewhere at the bottom of the sea. Somewhere in me.

Sometimes the light is strong enough to reach to the bottom of the sea.

'I think this is your coffee too,' I said.

You sat down and I noticed your hands – long fingers, articulated at the joints; if you touched me, what would happen?

I am shy with strangers – all those years alone on the rock with Pew. Our only visitor was Miss Pinch, and she was unrepresentative of the human race.

So now, when I meet someone new, I do the only thing I know how to do:

Tell you a story.

Pew

and I were sitting on the floor in front of the wood-burning stove. We were oiling and cleaning the movable parts of the instruments. Pew had unscrewed the brass knobs and sliding plates, lifted out the glass, and detached the delicate hands that hovered over the rising and falling of the sea and the wind.

At the beginning of every winter, he opened all the instrument cases, and loosened the threads of the screws and bolts, so that he could apply a single drop of transparent oil to clean their workings.

He had never needed to see what he was doing. Pews knew, he said, like fish swim. Lighthousekeeping was what Pews were born to do, and lighthousekeeping is what they did.

It had come about strangely, as you might have guessed, when old Josiah Dark was looking for his first man.

Whenever old Dark was in a tight place, he defied it by taking a walk. He had a belief that one kind of motion might encourage another. So, that day in Salts, he walked and he walked, and sure enough he met a man who collected spiders' webs.

The first thing Josiah noticed about the man was his fingers: long like a spider's legs, and articulated at the joints. The man was lifting webs from the hedgerows and stretching them inside a frame he had cut from hedgerow timber. He had invented a way of preserving the webs, and he sold them for good money to sailors who wanted a curiosity for their women at home.

'What's your name?' said Josiah.

'Pew.'

'Where's your lodging?'

'Here, there, not here and not there, and seasonally elsewhere.'

'Have you a wife?'

'Not that would know me in the daylight.'

So it was settled, and Pew, with his active fingers and quick ways, became the first lighthousekeeper at Cape Wrath.

'He wasn't blind though, Pew, was he?'

'No he wasn't, child, but that's not the end of the story.'

'Well then …'

'Well then, long after Josiah was gone, and soon after Babel was dead, there was another visitor to Salts. Not Molly O'Rourke this time, but her first child, Susan Lux, the child born blind at birth.

'Nobody knows why she came – but she never left again. She married Pew, in spite of their difference in age and upbringing – him all in the hedge, and her in a proper house, and him old enough to be her father, and her young enough to believe all the stories he told her. She had fingers quick as his, and soon his eyes were as blue and milky as hers. He became blind as he grew older, but they neither of them had any difficulty with that, what with senses as fine as a spider and hands that could hang a web.

'Their child was the same. And every Pew since. One or many, as you like it. Blind Pew Lighthousekeeping.'

'What about me?'

'What about you?'

'I'm not blind.'

'You have the handicap of sight, it's true.'

'So how will I keep the light?'

Pew smiled as he slotted the glass back into the tight rim of the barometer.

'Never rely on what you can see. Not everything can be seen.'

I looked out at the waves and the ships and the birds.

'Now close your eyes,' said Pew, who knew what I was

doing. I closed my eyes. He took my hand, his fingers curling round me like a net.

'What can you see now?'

'I can see Babel Dark coming towards the lighthouse.'

'What else can you see?'

'I can see me, but I look old.'

'What else can you see?'

'I can see you in a blue boat, but you look young.'

'Open your eyes.'

I opened my eyes, and saw the waves and the ships and the birds. Pew let go of my hand. 'Now you know what to do.'

THE HUT

This is a love story.

When I fell in love with you, I invited you to stay in a hut on the edge of a forest. Solitary, field-flung, perched over the earth, and hand-lit, it was the nearest thing I could get to a lighthouse.

Every new beginning prompts a return.

You were taking a boat, a plane, a train and a car to get this far from Hydra. Your exotic travel done, we were going to meet at a carwash near the station.

I tried to get everything ready for you – piled up the wood for the stove, found candles, made the bed with a new sheet I had bought, shelled beans into a pot, and put the steak under a cloth to keep the flies away. I had an old radio with me, because they were broadcasting *Tristan* that night, and I wanted to listen to it with you, drinking red wine and watching the night begin.

I was so early to meet you that I had to wash the car

twice, so that the suspicious Indian wouldn't send me away. Maybe he thought I was dealing drugs; the car was silver, like me, and a bit flash, and obviously I had got it by being up to no good. I tried to be friendly to him and bought a Mars Bar, but he just sat behind the desk reading the price lists in *Auto Trader*, to see how much I was making from my life of crime.

I paced up and down, like people do in suspense movies. Where were you? The mini-cab bringing you from the station would be hard to spot. Every car that slowed down for the Drive-In Macdonald's got the once-over twice over. I was like a Customs official. You were smuggled goods. I was supposed to be staying at the hut. You weren't.

At last, when I had polished my car so shiny that signals from outer space were bouncing off the bonnet, I saw a maroon Rover slow down towards me. You got out of the back. I rushed to pay the driver, scattering £10 notes like breadcrumbs.

I was too shy to kiss you.

The hut was made of rough brown planks, bark-topped, that overlapped under a clay tile roof. It had no foundations; it stood two metres off the ground on a set of staddle stones. This kept the rats away, but the night-time creatures snuffled and shuffled underneath.

That first night, in the unsteady single bed, I lay awake while you slept. I was listening to the unfamiliar noises, and thinking about the miracle of the most unfamiliar of them all – you breathing next to me.

I had fried the steaks. You had opened the bottle of St Amour, and we drank it out of thick old-fashioned tooth glasses. We had the door open, and the fire in the stove was making patterns on the floor. Outside, the moon was shadowing the grass, and the first sounds of the night-forest were beginning.

I was hungry, but I was nervous too. You were so new and I didn't want to frighten you away. I didn't want to frighten myself away.

Breathe in. Breathe out. Your rhythm different to mine. Your body not mine; the celebrated strangeness of another. I put my head against your chest, and it must have been something to do with the vibrations of the hut, because underneath your breathing, or through it, I could hear a badger breathing too.

The hut was breath: the narrow air-flow of the stove where the low fire was burning down; the quiet hiss of water heating in the big kettle on the stove's top; the draught through the key-hole rattling the heavy bolt-chain; the wind like a mouth-organ.

I put my mouth on yours, and your breathing changed as you kissed me in your sleep. I lay down, my hand on your stomach, following the rise and fall of another land.

The following morning, I woke early, stiff and thirsty, because no one sleeps well in a small bed with a not so small lover. My bed at the lighthouse had been tiny, but I only had to share it with DogJim.

I think I had spent the night with you balanced in the six-inch gap between the edge of the bed and the tongue-and-groove wall. You were lying centre square, your head on both pillows, snoring. I didn't want to wake you, so I just slid down the six-inch gap, and crawled out under the bed, bringing with me a very dusty almanac for 1932.

I pulled on a sweater and opened the door. The air was white and heavy. Everything was wet. There was a smell of ploughing. It was autumn and they were turning in the straw-stubble.

I looked back at you. These moments that are talismans and treasure. Cumulative deposits – our fossil record – and the beginnings of what happens next.

They are the beginning of a story, and the story we will always tell.

I tiptoed to the stove and took the heavy iron kettle outside. I poured some of it into a shallow bowl and mixed it with cold water from our plastic jerry can. I had a plant pot to hold my soap and shampoo, and I hung my towel on a useful hook gouged into one of the supporting posts of the hut. Then I took off all my clothes and started pouring water over my head. The water poured over me like sunlight. I thought of you in Hydra, strong as sunlight, and as free.

I dried myself on a rough blue towel. Clean, in clean clothes, with my lungs cleaned by the moist air, I woke you up to boiling coffee and bacon and eggs. You were sleepy and slow, and sat half-dozing in my dressing gown on the steps, shivering a bit in the late-year sun.

I love your skin; skin like breath, moving and sweet. When I touch you, your skin shivers twice, but not with this cold dawn.

You did the washing-up, singing, and then we went into town to buy chops and champagne. We were so happy that happiness went with us, and I charmed a toilet attendant into charging your mobile phone. We bought him a big tin of Cadbury's Roses, and he said he'd take them to his wife who had Alzheimer's.

'It was the aluminium saucepans,' he said. 'We didn't know any better then.'

I was holding your hand while he talked. There is so little life, and it is fraught with chance. We meet, we don't meet, we take the wrong turning, and still bump into each other. We conscientiously choose the 'right road' and it leads nowhere.

'I'm sorry,' I said to him.

'Thanks for these,' he said, holding them up. 'She'll love these.'

We drove to Ironbridge – birthplace of the Industrial Revolution. The light was lengthening in soft lines along the river. Whether it was the quality of light, or the clarity of my feelings for you, I don't know, but there was softness and no blurring. 'This is not a lie,' I said to myself. 'It may not hold, but it is true.'

We stood on the bridge looking down the wide river. I imagined the iron coal-carts on their iron wheels running on a pulley up and down the iron rails, fuelling the steam-sheds and turning the pistons of the engines that were still beautiful as well as useful. The black sharp smell of oiled iron filled these sheds. The floor was thick with filings. The noise was deafening.

The river was past and future. It flowed the barges, carried the goods, provided water power and cooling power, dredged away the effluent with cheerful grace, and at night made a haunt for the manual workers turned fishermen, who stood half screened on the bank at the end of their shift.

Their clothes were heavy, their hands had torn and healed. They shared tobacco and passed round a stone bottle of homemade beer. They kept maggots in a worn washer tin. There were trout in the river if you knew where to wait.

You were walking ahead of me over the bridge. 'Wait!' I called, and you turned round, smiling, and bent your head to kiss me. I looked back, half sorry to leave my world of shadows, as real as the real world. Yes, the men were there all right, fishing, smoking, loosening their neck cloths to wipe their faces. The one they called George was quiet because his wife had got pregnant again. He couldn't afford another child. But he could do an extra shift, if his body could stand it.

I felt his anxiety in the cold fog now beginning to rise from the river. So many lives – layered and layered, and easy to find, if you are quiet enough, and know where to wait, and coax them like trout.

I asked you to go over to the pub and see if they would sell us some ice for our champagne. You came back carrying a black bin liner with an Eskimo winter inside. 'He dug it out of a walk-in freezer with a spade,' you said, and then because my car had only two seats, you had to sit with it on your knee all the way back to the hut. 'This is love,' you said, and I know you were joking, but I hoped you meant it.

At the hut, I lit all the candles, then lay on the floor and blew air into the stove. You were chopping vegetables and telling me about a day in Thailand when you had seen turtles hatch in the sand. Not many of them make it to the sea, and once there, the sharks are waiting for them. Days disappear and get swallowed up much like that, but the ones like these, the ones that make it, swim out and return for the rest of your life.

Thank you for making me happy.

We were standing up in the near-dark. I had my hands on your hips, yours were on my shoulders. When we kiss, I stand on tiptoe. You are very good for my calves.

You slipped me out of my shirt, and began to touch my breasts through my bra, which is soft and tight over

216

my nipples. You said something about the bed, and we lay down, you kicking off your undone trainers and linen trousers, your legs brown and bare.

For a long time, we were side by side, stroking, not speaking, and then you ran your index finger down my nose, and into my mouth. You pushed me under you, kissing me, finding the channel of my body, finding me wet.

We were moving together; you turned me over, covering me from behind, craning your neck to reach round and kiss me, licking the sweat from my upper lip. I love the weight of you, and how you use it to pleasure me. I love your excitement. I love it that you don't ask me or hesitate. At the last possible second, you lifted me right up and pushed between my legs.

Then you were down on me, your tongue in the folds of me, your hands over my breasts, making me arch to follow you, you following me, until I had come.

I couldn't wait. I put you on your back, sitting across you, watching your eyes closed and your head turned to the side, your hands guiding me, and the movement of you so certain.

You are beautiful to feel. Beautiful inside me me inside you. Beautiful body making geometry out of our separate shapes.

We both love kissing. We do a lot of it. Lying together now, unable to part. I fell asleep breathing you.

Some time in the night, I heard a noise outside. I tried to pull myself out of the heavy sex-sleep, because someone was coming in at the door. You woke too, and we lay there, hearts beating, wondering, not knowing. Then I couldn't stand the tension, so I just grabbed the dressing gown and opened the door.

On the steps that led up to the hut was the bin bag full of mostly melted ice and a floating bottle of champagne, like a relic from the *Titanic*. A baby badger had his head and body three-quarters of the way in the bag.

We helped him free and threw him a packet of biscuits, because badgers love biscuits, and then, because it seemed like an omen of celebration, we opened the champagne and got back into bed to drink it.

'How long do you think we've got?' you said.

'What, before we make love again, before we finish the champagne or before it's morning?'

I fell asleep, and dreamed of a door opening.

Doors opening into rooms that opened onto doors that opened into rooms. We burst through, panelled, baize, flush, glazed, steel, reinforced, safe doors, secret doors, double doors, trap doors. The forbidden door that can only be opened with a small silver key. The door that is no door in Rapunzel's lonely tower.

You are the door in the rock that finally swings free when moonlight shines on it. You are the door at the top of the stairs that only appears in dreams. You are the door that sets the prisoner free. You are the carved low door into the Chapel of the Grail. You are the door at the edge of the world. You are the door that opens onto a sea of stars.

Open me. Wide. Narrow. Pass through me, and whatever lies on the other side, could not be reached except by this. This you. This now. This caught moment opening into a lifetime.

His heart was beating like light.

Dark was walking on the headland. The light flashing every four seconds as it always had. His body was timed to it.

The sea and the sky were black, but the light opened the water like a fire was burning there.

'You did that for me,' he said, though there were no listeners, only bladderwrack and poppies. 'You opened the water like a fire.'

He had been walking most of the night. If he didn't walk, he lay awake. He preferred to walk.

That day in the lighthouse ... and she had gone. Some weeks later a letter had arrived for him, and with the letter, a ruby and emerald pin. He knew he would never see her again.

All those years – all those years ago, and he had doubted her. Their child Susan was three before she had told him that the man he believed to be her lover was her brother. A smuggler, a fugitive, but still her brother.

Why had he listened to Price? Why had he trusted a man who was a blackmailer and a thief?

But all that had been forgiven. He had betrayed her a second time.

He breathed in, wanting the cold night air, but it was salt water he breathed. His body was filled with salt water. He was drowned already. He no longer came up for air. He floated underneath the world and heard its voices strange and far-off. He rarely understood what people said. He was aware of vague shapes passing across him. Nothing more.

Then, sometimes, floating face up in his underwater cave, a memory so bright hit him, like the flat of a sword, that the water opened, and he felt his face rush up for air, and he gulped air, and in the night, all around him, were the stars lying on water. He kicked them with his upturned feet. He was patterned in stars.

The water poured off his face, his hair streamed back. He wasn't dying any more. She was there. She had come back.

He had the seahorse in his pocket. Time's frail hero. One more journey left to make.

They waded out, they swam, they swam into the cone of light, that sank down like a dropped star. The light shaft was deeper than he had expected, signalling the way to the bottom of the world. His body was weightless now. His mind was clear. He would find her.

He let the seahorse go. He held out his hands.

Tell me a story, Silver.

What story?
This one.

Part broken part whole, you begin again.

The tour was filing dutifully down the stairs. The guide looked back to make sure we were all following, and at the moment he turned forward, I took out my little silver key and opened the door into our kitchen.

Silently, I closed it and locked myself in. Far away, I heard the guide shutting up the lighthouse.

We had been allowed to peer in, one by one, to the makeshift kitchen where Pew and I had eaten herds of sausages. The dented brass kettle was unpolished on the wood-burning stove. The comb-backed Windsor chair, where Pew used to sit, was in the corner. My stool was neat against the wall.

'It was a hard and lonely life,' the guide had said, 'with few comforts.'

'How did they cook on that thing?' asked one of the tour.

'A microwave is not a passport to happiness,' I said, snappish.

Everyone glared at me.

I didn't care. I had made my plan.

The lighthouse was open to the public twice a year. Finally, not knowing what I did, I had come back.

Now, listening to the diesel-drone of the tour bus pulling away, I was alone. I half expected DogJim to come trotting through the door.

I pulled out the stool and sat down. How quiet it was without the clock ticking. I got up, opened the drawer under the clock-face, took out the key and wound the spring. Tick, tick, tick. Better – much better. Time had begun again.

The stove had rusted red round the handle. I forced it free and looked inside. Twenty years ago I had left in the early morning and laid a fire, because that's what I always did. The fire was still there, unlit, but still there. I knocked back the spigot that opened the tin vent of the flue. A shower of dust and rust fell down, but I could feel from the rush of air that the vent was clear. I put a match to the dry kindling and paper. The fire roared up. I grabbed the kettle as the condensation began to mist on it in the heat. I swilled it out with water, filled it up, and made myself a twenty-year-old pot of tea. Full Strength Samson.

The light was thinning, losing colour, turning transparent. The day had worn through and the stars were showing.

I took my mug of tea and climbed up past Pew's room to the control room, and out onto the deck that ran all the way round the Light.

I leaned on the rail and looked out. Every four minutes the light flashed in a single clear beam, visible across the sea and across the sea of time too.

I had often seen this light. Inland, land-locked, sailing my years, uncertain of my position, the light had been what Pew had promised – marker, guide, comfort and warning.

Then I saw him. Pew in the blue boat.

'Pew!' Pew!'

He lifted his hand, and I ran down the steps and out onto the jetty, and there he was tying the painter as he always did, his shapeless hat pulled over his eyes.

'I wondered when you'd get here,' he said.

Pew: Unicorn. Mercury. Lenses. Levers. Stories. Light.

There has always been a Pew at Cape Wrath. But not the same Pew?

We talked all night, as though we had never gone away, as though that broken day had been hinged onto this one, and the two folded together, back to back, Pew and Silver, then and now.

'Tell me a story,' said Pew.

'A book, a bird, an island, a hut, a small bed, a badger, a beginning ...'

'And did you tell that person what I told you?' said Pew.

'When you love someone you should say it.'

'That's right, child.'

'I did what you told me.'

'Well, well, that's good.'

'I love you, Pew.'

'What's that, child?'

'I love you.'

He smiled, his eyes like a faraway ship. 'I've a story for you too'

'What?'

'It was Miss Pinch who was the orphan.'

'Miss Pinch!'

'Never was a descendant of Babel Dark. Never forgave any of us for that.'

And I was back in Railings Row under the One-Duck Eiderdown, duck feathers, duck feet, duck bill, glassy duck eyes, and snooked duck tail, waiting for daylight.

We are lucky, even the worst of us, because daylight comes.

The fire was burning down, and there was a strange silence outside, as if the sea had stopped moving. Then we heard a dog barking.

'That's DogJim,' said Pew. 'Hark him.'

'Is he still alive?'

'He's still barking,'

Pew stood up. 'It will soon be daylight, Silver, and time to go.'

'Where are you going?'

Pew shrugged. 'Here, there, not here, not there, and seasonally elsewhere.'

'Will I see you again?'

'There's always been a Pew at Cape Wrath.'

I watched him get into the boat and align the tiller. DogJim was sitting up in the prow, wagging his tail. Pew began to row off the rocks, and at that moment the sun lifted, and shone through Pew and the boat. The light was so intense that I had to shade my eyes, and when I looked again, Pew and the boat were gone.

I stayed at the lighthouse until the day was done. As

I left, the sun was setting, and the full moon was rising on the other side of the sky. I stretched out my hands, holding the falling sun in one hand, and the climbing moon in the other, my silver and gold, my gift from life. My gift of life.

My life is a hesitation in time. An opening in a cave. A gap for a word.

These were my stories – flashes across time.

I'll call you, and we'll light a fire, and drink some wine, and recognise each other in the place that is ours. Don't wait. Don't tell the story later.

Life is so short. This stretch of sea and sand, this walk on the shore, before the tide covers everything we have done.

I love you.

The three most difficult words in the world.

But what else can I say?

Ideas,
interviews
& features . . .

About the author

About the book

Read on

From Innocence to Experience

Louise Tucker talks to Jeanette Winterson

OTHER WRITERS ARE referenced throughout *Lighthousekeeping*, as they often are in your work. Why is intertextuality so important to your writing?

Books speak to other books; they are always in dialogue. Books that we have now affect the way we read books that were written earlier, at any other period, because books are a continual commentary on themselves. This is one of the reasons why the process is always dynamic, not static, why it moves, why it's exciting for the reader and for the writer. I think everyone has the experience of building a private library, not just on the shelves but in their minds, where they're always comparing and contrasting new books that they've read with classics that they loved. For a writer that process is even sharper because you're dealing with words all the time and you are aware that you write within a continuum, that the books themselves suggest ideas to you which you might not otherwise have had.

I've always liked to work with existing texts. I like to do cover versions of stories that we know very well, whether it's Lancelot and Guinevere or Tristan and Isolde. It's a way of rewriting what we know, but in the rewriting we find new angles, new possibilities, and the rewriting itself demands an injection of fresh material into what already exists, so the story changes. The thing is kept alive by the retelling, by the changing. It's a way of making an oral tradition out of a literary tradition so that the thing is continuously in the mouth. I think words ought to be in the mouth; it's where they belong. The spoken language is just as important as the written language; the two depend on one another. I think of it not as a literary game, nor as an exercise, but as a necessary nourishment from one text to another.

You mention on your website that *The PowerBook* is the end of a cycle. Is *Lighthousekeeping* the beginning of a new one?
Yes it is. It's a new exploration. I don't know where it will lead, I don't know what comes next. I have no plans at present for another novel, but for me that's normal. I never plan ahead. I think it's necessary for writers always to be prepared to renew themselves and to reconsider the way that they work. I don't want to parody other people but I don't want to parody myself either, and nor do I want to start writing the same book, which can be a danger when you've been working for a while, and I've been working for twenty years now in 2005. So it's a question of letting new ideas come through and not being afraid of that and not being afraid of things ending, because out of those endings come the possibilities of new beginnings. I don't think there is any other way to work. ▶

> ❛ I have no plans at present for another novel, but for me that's normal. I never plan ahead. It's a question of letting new ideas come through and not being afraid of that. ❜

From Innocence to Experience *(continued)*

◄ *Lighthousekeeping* **revolves very specifically around telling stories. Why do you think storytelling, as an act, is so important to us?**

Storytelling is a way of establishing connections, imaginative connections for ourselves, a way of joining up disparate material and making sense of the world. Human beings love patterns; they love to see shapes and symmetries. We seem to have a need to impose order on our surroundings, which are generally chaotic and often in themselves seem to lack any continuity, any storyline. For me, though, the telling of stories is not about imposing an order, it's about revealing an order which is implicit in a situation but perhaps concealed, perhaps well hidden.

I believe in pattern and in order but I don't believe that those things are artificial. I think that art is one way of discovering a genuine and unforced pattern in our lives and in the world around us and that's why writing can never be formulaic: it can never be done according to plan because it arises from a deeper part of the self which I think is less neurotic than the conscious mind and less afraid of not immediately having a shape to put on every new situation. We can be obsessive, always wanting to categorise and quantify; we become taxonomists, and it's not always helpful. It's often better to let the pattern emerge in its own right. The pattern might be slightly flawed, the shape might be different to the one that we would imagine, but it's still valid, and storytelling allows that to happen. Nothing in the story ever quite

6 Art is one way of discovering a genuine and unforced pattern in our lives and in the world around us and that's why writing can never be formulaic. 9

works out in the way you imagine it will: there are always surprises, there are always twists and turns.

Storytelling teaches us to be unafraid of our imaginative power and I think it teaches us to be unafraid of the exuberance and the unruly, untamed nature of life, of our lives. So in a world which is obsessed with taming, obsessed with making sense of things – which often means reducing those things – stories are a way of making sense differently, of enlarging upon what we are and not being afraid of the unruly elements within it.

Many of your books cross boundaries of time and history. Do you spend a lot of time doing research before you start writing?
I pick up things that I need as I go along. I don't sit down and try and get everything into a neat pile next to my computer before I start. I think you have to let the work suggest its own conundrums and then you start to solve them. So when I need a piece of research I go out and get it. Otherwise I think you tend towards the formulaic, which I believe is unhelpful. If you think you know where the story will go, then you're perhaps directing it too much with your conscious mind. You need the story itself to suggest things to you.

I'm a great believer in working with the unconscious, working with those parts of the self which aren't immediately accessible to rationale or logic. After all, if art reaches anywhere it reaches underneath the surface of the everyday, it reaches past our logical decisions and reasons and it reaches into ▶

LIFE AT A GLANCE

Author photo:
Peter Peitsch/peitschphotos.com

BORN
Manchester, 1959.

EDUCATED
Accrington Girls' High School; St Catherine's College, Oxford.

LIVES
Oxfordshire and London.

BOOKS
Include *Oranges Are Not the Only Fruit*, *Written on the Body*, *The Passion*, *Sexing the Cherry* and *The PowerBook*.

From Innocence to Experience (*continued*)

◄ another place, which is richer, stranger, perhaps closer to the world of the child than to the world of the adult. I don't think we grow out of that world; I think we suppress it, ignore it and lose touch with it. Reading, looking at pictures, listening to music, going to the theatre, all of those things allow us to regain contact with the parts of our selves that growing up and living in this crazy, corporate world try to squeeze out.

Inevitably a high-profile writer's life and work are conflated. Do you find this irritating or simply par for the course?
My own writing life has run parallel to a change in the way that writers are perceived by the public and the media. Until the late eighties writers were much more anonymous. They were unlikely to be recognised; they might do one or two interviews but they were not in any sense treated as celebrities, nor were they expected to give opinions on the state of the world and generally air their views. This changed when the media realised that it could treat writers in this way and it would be entertaining because, unlike rock stars and actors, writers tend not to go around with PR people who warn them when to keep quiet and not to answer certain questions. So it's very easy to make us look ridiculous. Everybody's had a lot of fun with this. Writers have wised up now: we know how it's going to be so we're a lot more careful. Personally I think it's unhelpful that writers are treated as celebrities; I think it's better that we should be treated as nobodies and only the work

❝ I'm a great believer in working with the unconscious, working with those parts of the self which aren't immediately accessible to rationale or logic. ❞

should be on show, but that's never going to happen. So you have to live in the world that you're in; there's no point in lamenting for a lost Arcadia – it won't come back. My view is to cooperate now as much as I can and to try and keep private what I can.

I think questions of autobiography are always misleading because every writer uses themselves in their work; they use their own experience, they use what they observe, hopefully they use what they can imagine but perhaps that's less frequent than it ought to be. But really autobiography tells us very little. What we should be looking for is authenticity: if this comes from the centre of the writer, if it comes from a real place in the writer then that will show itself in the work. And I think it's authenticity we should be looking at, not autobiography. There's only so much the autobiography can tell us. But at present we are obsessed with writers' lives, with what we think of as true life, with what we think of as the real story. There is no real story, the real story is in the fiction.

What was it like to start, finish and sell *Oranges Are Not the Only Fruit*? What was that first book like?

It was entirely innocent. You really only get that for a couple of times in a writer's life because then you start to be out in the world, you become a published figure – the whole perspective changes. The innocence goes and your only hope then is to make a William Blake-style journey from innocence to experience. There is no other way to recover that particular joy and surprise that you ▶

7

◄ **What's your favourite trashy read?**
I don't really have a reading one but I do listen to *The Archers*. ■

◄ get in your work right at the beginning. Trudging through the middle period can be rather dreary. I have got the joy and surprise back now but it has been a very particular journey.

Thinking back on *Oranges*, it was done in the heat of enthusiasm; it was done without consideration for what anyone might think, without looking over my shoulder, without hesitation. I had nothing to lose, I had everything to gain, it was very free. Inevitably that changes. I was surprised that it did as well as it did. It shouldn't have because it was only published in paperback and it didn't get any marketing behind it, but it began to move under its own momentum and the rest of the story is, I think, well known.

***Oranges* was enormously successful both as a book and as a television series. None of your other books has been televised. Would you want them to be?**
I wouldn't particularly. I enjoyed doing *The PowerBook* for the stage, for instance, but although television is very persuasive because everyone watches it and you hope that then they'll buy the book – well, publishers do because then they make lots of money – it's not something I feel is particularly necessary. For me the pleasure is the book and the books are what I want to write. So it may happen but I don't really care either way.

***Boating for Beginners* is often dismissed whereas it is in fact a very funny, very enjoyable book. Does it annoy you that it**

doesn't get as much press as some of your other books, that it's a lost book?
No, if it's a lost book it is because, I have let it be lost simply because although I'm very fond of it, it is what it is. It's a particular kind of comic book and I didn't put myself into it in the way that I have done with my other books because I didn't take it seriously. It was written very quickly, it was written in six weeks and it was just to fund me. I didn't have any money in those days and I was asked to do it for the humour list for Methuen at the time and I thought, 'Why not?' It was at the time that I was writing my fitness book and I would do anything just to keep myself going. I'm a writer, I hope I'm a good writer – if not, everybody's been conned for the last twenty years – but that means you can turn your hand to anything. I often think of myself as running a little workshop: I make things to sell, I'm not precious about it. I feel that I can pretty much write anything that anybody wants me to write because that's the professional side of it, the skill side of it, and then there are the things you do because you put your heart into them.

Do you have a favourite book of yours?
No, they all occupy particular spaces. To some extent it's like looking back on your old record collection, or diaries that you don't read any more. You were there, you were that person, they meant everything to you at the time. But you move past them, you are somebody else, you become somebody else because of writing the book. The books are ▶

❢ My own writing life has run parallel to a change in the way that writers are perceived by the public and the media. ❢

◄ your tutors and your guide: they make you as much as you make them. But then they are absorbed at the level of familiarity because they're in your DNA and at the same time, which is a paradox, they're absolutely strange. I look on the shelf – in a bookshop somewhere – and think, 'Oh, I wrote those', and that's always a little bit of a surprise.

Your website not only supplies information about your own work but also that of many other writers, especially poets. Would you say that poetry is something that influences you, or that you are trying to achieve, and would you ever consider writing it?
I wouldn't consider writing it, no. Poetry is the thing that matters to me more than anything else. I use it like caffeine: when I'm tired I'll have a shot of poetry. I always carry it with me; I look for that exactness of language, that sensitivity and feeling. But I won't write it because I have decided that my experiment is to use those poetic disciplines and work them against the stretchiness of narrative. It may be a foolish experiment in a world that speed-reads – although I only write short books, they don't lend themselves to being read very quickly. The sentences matter, every word in every sentence is made to matter, it's not simply about conveying information. I try to do more than that. So it's absolute anathema to the idea of reading six books a day leaning against the fridge, as I believe they do for the Booker Prize!

I don't have any plans to produce a book of poetry but, who knows, that may change. I think poets and poetry are having a

6 I think it's unhelpful that writers are treated as celebrities; we should be treated as nobodies and only the work should be on show. 9

renaissance at the moment – people understand perhaps better than they have done for a long time what poetry is and that it matters; there's room for it in people's lives now. That's a good thing.

When discussing your editions of Virginia Woolf, you mention how much you dislike literary criticism, especially critical theory. How does it feel, as a writer, to appear on syllabuses the world over?
We get a lot of emails on the site saying, 'I'm doing this or that essay', meaning 'Can you write it for me?' The answer is no! It entertains me, and again it's one of the things that I'm surprised by, that I'm there and being taught. I think you have to leave people alone to work out their own interpretations. I don't mind what people write about my work and I don't read it because there's no need to read it. I think you have to allow the thing to go on its own way and collect whatever it wants along the way without worrying too much or saying, 'I didn't mean that.' It's redundant for a writer to say, 'That's not what I meant' or, 'I meant something else.' The text lives outside of that very simplistic space.

Of course it's always difficult when one's alive; it's much easier when you're dead! I think the whole critical push for the death of the author was really wishful thinking on the part of the critics who longed for it. If criticism brings people to think about books, if it helps them to formulate their own thoughts and to read more then it's a good thing, always a good thing. I think now that there's so much pressure put on people to ▶

> ❝ I often think of myself as running a little workshop: I make things to sell, I'm not precious about it. ❞

From Innocence to Experience *(continued)*

◄ produce papers, for academics to write books, the work must end up being poor quality and rather low grade, which is a pity for everyone. Nobody wins in that situation. You should only write about things that you love and where you feel that you've got something to contribute, and of course that's not fashionable any more. I had some A-level students emailing me the other day to ask, 'What did you mean in *Oranges* by the "rough brown pebble"?' and I thought, 'Oh, I have no idea!' I'm going to come up with something for them, I must have meant something, mustn't I?!

Your shop opening received a lot of press coverage. What inspired you to open it, and is it in any way a distraction?
Well, I don't run the shop. It's a fantasy of the media that I am to be found there selling olives and Parmesan cheese. I've never sold an olive in my life and I don't intend to start selling one now. I own the building and it's right that there should be a shop and I wanted the kind of shop that I like to shop in. I didn't want cushions and candles, a lifestyle shop, and I didn't want to sell out to a corporation doing coffee or plastic sandwiches. I wanted a real shop and I wanted a beautiful shop. I wanted to know that when I come to London I can pick up my supper and take it upstairs and eat it. It was a great muddle of altruism, high-mindedness, selfishness and 'I'll do this because I can'. So I did.

You write journalism, columns, have edited Virginia Woolf and now own a shop. When

❛ I look on the shelf – in a bookshop somewhere – and think, 'Oh, I wrote those', and that's always a little bit of a surprise. ❜

do you have time or space to think about writing your next book?

I'm thinking all the time. I don't think that ever stops except when I'm in the gym. In fact one of the reasons that I go to the gym is because I can stop thinking there, which is an enormous relief.

I'm not a New Yorker by temperament; I'm not a frenzied person who only sleeps four hours a night and thinks she has to put everything in and that's the way to live a perfect life – not at all. But I do think that it's right to put as much into life as you can and to get as much out of life as you can. Of course that includes doing things slowly and doing things well – finding time for your friends, cooking properly, reading, going for walks, playing – all of the things which apparently yield no results. You don't make money that way and you don't get on in life that way, but what you get is something much more important. You get space for your mind. We don't have a lot of that and of course you can't believe in art in the way that I do and not believe that people need space for the mind, to slow down and to find time.

People are always saying that they haven't got time for anything: I think there is time, but it demands prioritising and it demands rethinking the way we live our lives. So I just make sure that I take time: I walk every day, I think about things, I read, I let things come up from that deep place that I talk about. You have to find time for that still small voice. Some people do it by meditation, I do it by switching the phone off, going out and being by myself with my own thoughts. ▶

> ❝ I do think that it's right to put as much into life as you can and to get as much out of life as you can. That includes doing things slowly and doing things well. ❞

From Innocence to Experience *(continued)*

◄ **Do you know what your next book will be yet?**
No idea. I'm doing a children's book for Bloomsbury which will be published next year. I'm not thinking about any other projects until I've finished it.

Top Ten Books

THESE ARE NOT in any order of preference. I have had to miss out all the plays I love to read, and so many of the poets, but this is a representative choice, and an honest one. In an ideal world I would have added the Bible and the *Collected Works* of Jung, plus loads of art books by old fogies like Roger Fry, Clive Bell and Kenneth Clark. As it is, my top ten has stretched to eleven, and I haven't got in any of the exciting thinkers, like Susan Sontag.

Invisible Cities
Italo Calvino
The perfect anti-realism, short-form narrative. An antidote to those big fat documentary novels that pretend to be a slice of life.

Wuthering Heights
Emily Brontë
Wild, driven, uncouth, poetic. This is not Jane Austen's rigorous admirable style or George Eliot's magisterial narrative, or Charlotte Brontë's contained explosions. *Wuthering Heights* is untamed. True feral energy for the first time in fiction by a woman.

Orlando
Virginia Woolf
What a carve-up! Such a daring thing to do in 1928. Here is the boldness of a fiction masquerading as a biography, a woman masquerading as a man. She smuggles across the borders of propriety the most outrageous contraband – same-sex love, time travel, ▶

◄ shape-shifting, a revision of history. All the things we have come to take for granted from modern fiction, including the collapse of genres, begin here. It is Woolf's finest achievement, as well as her most popular novel.

Finn Family Moomintroll
Tove Jansson

All of the Moomin books have to go in here for their celebration of imagination and the richness of their fantasy. Moominland is a complete world and one that challenges the dreariness of ours. I still read them sitting on the loo in my study. I love them.

The Inferno
Dante

A strong dark poem, as urgent in feel as it was when Dante wrote it six centuries ago. Which of us has not felt ourselves alone in a dark wood? That *selva oscura* of the soul? The best English translation is the 2002 text by the Belfast poet Ciaran Carson – a really fabulous piece of work, as chewy in the mouth as Dante's original.

Four Quartets
T.S. Eliot

This poem means so much to me, in what it has to say and in the way that it says it. A great poem is a journey inwards, and when I am bruised with too much of life's outward show, I come back here, for quiet and for energy, because in art, quiet and energy are found in the same place.

The Thing in the Gap Stone Stile/Dart
Alice Oswald
Alice Oswald is such an exciting new poet.
When I first read her, the hairs on the back of
my neck stood on end. She is the real thing,
and that is what we need in a world of
makeshift and fake.

Tom Jones
Henry Fielding
Beautiful language, very funny, very sad, and
a reminder of the exuberance of eighteenth-
century writing – great freedom of
expression, and a very different sensibility to
the Victorians.

Sons and Lovers
D.H. Lawrence
What a good writer he is. I love his anger, his
sensuality, his prose like a powerful animal.

Venice
Jan Morris
Jan Morris has taken travel writing to new
continents of thought. I have enjoyed
everything she has written but I have a
special affection for this book because it fired
me to write a book of my own, *The Passion*
(1987), before I had been to Venice myself.

Letters to a Young Poet
Rilke
Read it and re-read it. I keep a copy in a my
travel bag. ∎

Endless Possibilities

By Jeanette Winterson

WHY WRITE A book about a child growing up in a lighthouse?
The answer would have to begin: Why write a book at all?

After I had finished my novel *The PowerBook*, published in 2000, I had a strong sense of a cycle of work ending. That cycle began with *Oranges Are Not the Only Fruit* in 1985, and felt more like a carpet I was weaving than a series of separate texts. I would cut the thread at the end of a book, only to take up the strands again, continuing a pattern, working new symbols, testing the symmetry, but with a sense of returning to work rather than starting again.

At the same time, I have never believed that writing one book will guarantee that I will write any more. I am a writer; that is how I identify myself, how I explain myself, how I dream myself, but I know that books cannot be forced. I know that the process is mysterious, and that those who try and explain it in practical terms – go on a creative writing course, plan your work, etc. – miss the real point of it all, that it rises from a deep place in the self, which does not yield to entreaty.

You may want to write a book, you may long to write a book, you may even force yourself to write a book, or worse, force a book to be written, but that is not the same thing as letting the book surface. Until it does, whatever you do will be an act of will, and not an act of imagination.

Creativity is not an amalgam of hard work and cleverness, or of hard work and sincerity, or of hard work and sleight of hand. Now that the use of the word 'creative' belongs to accountancy and advertising, and is also used as a badge of honour by media people at desk jobs, we forget that creativity is the most elusive of happenings. If it is happening, hard work and long hours are essential; if it is not happening, all we are doing is putting in overtime.

So I wait and I wait. Then I write and I write. Then I throw most of it away and start again.

I do not write sequentially because I do not think sequentially. I think in pictures, I think of bars of text, like bars of music. I think in scenes, like the cinema, or in voices, like the stage. I never think in terms of a beginning, a middle, an end.

I usually begin a book with a single sentence or a single image.

In the case of *Lighthousekeeping*, it was the opening sentence, 'My mother called me Silver. I was born part precious metal, part pirate.'

I knew that a whole character was packed in that sentence, and I set out to unpack her, and to see what would happen.

Some way through the book I sat down to work one morning, and simply typed in, 'He was walking his dog along the cliff path . . .' I stopped. What man? What dog? I realised that a new voice had broken through, and ▶

> 6 I usually begin a book with a single sentence or a single image. In the case of *Lighthousekeeping*, it was the opening sentence. 9

Endless Possibilities *(continued)*

◀ this turned out to be Babel Dark, the nineteenth-century clergyman struggling with demons of his own.

Of course there must be a strong critical and editorial process at work when you are writing – the thing is not an exercise in dictation from the Unconscious, but it is a delicate balance between unruly and unedited thoughts and feelings, and the necessary toughness to cut and discard and revise.

Only at the very end do I number the pages.

Lighthousekeeping is a story about telling stories. A story about what stories are, and how they affect us. Pew calls them 'markers, guides, comfort, and warning'.

I believe that. I believe that storytelling is a way of navigating our lives, and that to read ourselves as fiction is much more liberating than to read ourselves as fact. Facts are partial. Fiction is a more complete truth. If we read ourselves as narrative, we can change the story that we are. If we read ourselves as literal and fixed, we find we can change nothing. Someone will always tell the story of our lives – it had better be ourselves.

I wanted to pile stories on top of stories, like bedcovers for a cold night. At the same time, I wanted to break the obvious narrative, and not get bogged down in too much straight-line chronology. I wanted the reader to swing between one story and another, across time, and across character. Fiction is a leap of faith.

> ❛ *Lighthouse-keeping* is a story about telling stories. A story about what stories are, and how they affect us. ❜

Leaping takes energy, from the reader and from the writer, and we are living in a time when fiction is becoming more like a guided tour, a documentary, as close to 'real life' as possible, a mimic, a recording angel.

I am unsure that this is the best use of fiction.

Picasso was excited when photography began its serious work in the early twentieth century, because he thought it would finally free up painting from the burden of representation. I hoped that the narrative naturalism of film, and television in particular, would free up the novel from its dreary burden of 'life as it is lived', and allow it the talismanic and imaginative possibilities of poetry, where language, and ambition for the form itself, would be more important, more interesting, than everyday narrative.

Of course, all writers defend the kind of books they themselves write. I set out from the beginning to merge the exactness of poetic language with the stretchiness of storytelling. Sometimes I succeed, sometimes I don't. As Sam Beckett advised, 'Fail, fail again, fail better.'

I love words and my aim is to use them precisely, so that they become an equivalent to the feeling. So that the feeling can be spoken. All art is about emotion.

Lighthousekeeping.
The final section opens with the line 'Part broken, part whole, you begin again.'

It is a story, it is a net of stories, about beginnings. The hero, Silver, who I won't call a heroine because that word has a different ▶

> 6 I believe that storytelling is a way of navigating our lives, and that to read ourselves as fiction is much more liberating than to read ourselves as fact. 9

◀ loading, and no mythic status, must begin her life many times over. It is those moments of beginning, rather than their consequences, that she chooses to tell.

Our mental processes are more like a maze than a motorway. We do not remember our lives chronologically, nor do we reflect on them in neat order. We roam the labyrinths of our experiences, sometimes trying to find the way out, sometimes trying to find the centre, always a little bit lost unless some unexpected insight shows us the way.

Such insights are by their nature imaginative, poetic, heightened, revelatory. They are not the everyday accumulation of data.

Lighthousekeeping is about those moments – whether or not we act on them. The stories here are those moments that stop the clock as time ticks on. The moments we remember in our lives dedicated to forgetting.

Lighthousekeeping is a sea story, a love story, a loss story, a lost story, a life story, a bedtime story and my story.

That is, it is the only story I could tell at the time I wrote it. I might have preferred to write another story, but I could not do so.

I am not Silver and Silver is not I, but I am not separate from my work either – how could I be, when the stories are spun out of me spider-style?

They come from the centre, and while questions of autobiography are misleading and unhelpful, questions of authenticity are not. We cannot demand that writers write

> 6 We do not remember our lives chronologically, nor do we reflect on them in neat order. We roam the labyrinths of our experiences. 9

particular kinds of books (though that is what the marketplace and reviewers often do), and we cannot demand that writers write in the way we might prefer them to do (laments about the State of Fiction, blah blah). All we can ask is that the work should be authentic; that is, it should be true to the writer, true to language, true to the necessary development of the form, and true to itself.

Those are the kind of books I want to read, and so those are the kind of books I want to write.

That said, the possibilities are endless. ■

Have You Read?
Other novels by Jeanette Winterson

Oranges Are Not the Only Fruit

This is the story of Jeanette, adopted by working-class evangelists in the North of England in the sixties. Brought up to preach the gospel alongside such spiritual giants as Testifying Elsie and Pastor Spratt, Jeanette is destined for the missionary field, but her high success rate of converts turns into a charismatic encounter with one girl in particular. Love and sex were not scheduled into her timetable, but at sixteen Jeanette decides to leave the church, her home and her family for the young woman she loves. Funny and tender, *Oranges* is a document of the wilder side of religious enthusiasm, and an exploration of the power of love.

Boating for Beginners

'Do you understand the meaning of life?' asked Gloria. She knew that everyone sought this mysterious meaning because it was in all the magazines. Every month there was an article on how to be fulfilled and what to invest in when you were . . .

Boating for Beginners is the story of Noah and the Flood and a romantic novelist called Bunny Mix – the rabbit of romance. It's full of silly things and great fun.

The Passion

This is the story of Henri, a young Frenchman sent to fight in the Napoleonic wars. It is the story of Villanelle, a cross-dressing Venetian woman, born with webbed feet. There are four sections: The Emperor, The Queen of Spades,

The Zero Winter, The Rock. Told in the first person, The Emperor is Henri's narrative, while The Queen of Spades belongs to Villanelle. The pair meet in Russia in The Zero Winter. From then the narratives switch and intertwine. *The Passion* is about war, and the private acts that stand against war. It is about survival and broken-heartedness, and cruelty and madness.

Sexing the Cherry
This is the story of Jordan, an orphan found floating on the River Thames, and his keeper, the Dog Woman, a huge and monstrous creature with a powerful right hook and a wide vocabulary. She is perhaps the only woman in English fiction confident enough to use filth as a fashion accessory. The central relationship between Jordan and the Dog Woman is a savage love, an unorthodox love; it is family life carried to the grotesque, but it is not a parody or a negative. The boisterous surrealism of their bond is in the writing itself. *Sexing the Cherry* is a cross-time novel in the same way that *The Passion* is cross-gender. The narrative moves through time, but also operates outside it.

Written on the Body
A simple story: love found, love lost, love found again – maybe. The unnamed narrator falls for a married woman called Louise. Louise leaves her husband but when she finds she has cancer she leaves her new lover too. *Written on the Body* is a journey of self-discovery made through the metaphors of desire and disease. ▶

25

Have You Read? *(continued)*

◄ The PowerBook

An e-writer called Ali, or Alix (because x marks the spot), will pin up a story for you, cut it to fit. She is a language costumier, writing to order, letting you be the hero of your own life, offering you freedom just for one night. The price? Risk. You risk entering the story as yourself and leaving it as someone else. But if the narrative changes, then so does the narrator, as Ali discovers this is a price she too will have to pay. ■

Find Out More

READ. . .

To the Lighthouse; The Waves
Virginia Woolf

The Strange Case of Dr Jekyll and Mr Hyde
Robert Louis Stevenson

Life of Pi
Yann Martel

The Odyssey
Homer

The Passion of New Eve
Angela Carter

Like Water for Chocolate
Laura Esquivel

Landing Light
Don Paterson

Ground Water
Matthew Hollis

VISIT . . .

Cape Wrath
The location of Silver's lighthouse is the most
northwesterly part of the British mainland. It
can be reached by ferry and minibus. The
website, **www.capewrath.org.uk**, has lots of
pictures, local and lighthouse information.

The Museum of Scottish Lighthouses
Kinnaird Head, Stevenson Road, ▶

Find Out More *(continued)*

◄ Fraserburgh, AB43 9DU,
www.lighthousemuseum.co.uk
Kinnaird Head, the first lighthouse built on
top of a fortified castle, is now the home of
this museum and it has been kept as it was
when the last lighthousekeeper left.

SURF . . .

www.jeanettewinterson.com
A comprehensive site, produced by the
author, with information on each book as
well as her other writings. Also includes
reading suggestions and a bookshop.

**www.nlb.org.uk/ourlights/history/
capewrath.htm**
The Northern Lighthouses Board's website
has lots of historical and practical
information, including a page on each of the
lighthouses for which it is responsible
including this one for Cape Wrath
Lighthouse.

www.nts.org.uk
Stay in a Scottish lighthouse. The National
Trust for Scotland's website has links to the
various lighthouses and keepers' cottages
available for holiday lets.

LISTEN . . .

Tristan und Isolde
Richard Wagner ■